HEART QUAKE

Dr K. Vijayakarthikeyan is a medico-turned-bureaucrat well known for his hugely popular initiatives as an IAS officer. He has won several awards and accolades for his pioneering work in land, solid waste and urban management.

He has authored the national bestseller, *Once Upon an IAS Exam*, as well as five Tamil bestsellers, *Ettum Dhoorathil IAS*, *Adhuvum Idhuvum*, *Orey Kallil 13 Maanghai*, *Jeyippadhu Yeppadi* and *Oru Cup Coffee Saapidalama*. On sunny weekends, he can be found wreaking havoc on the cricket ground with his explosive batting and deceptive spin.

Reach him at:
Facebook: facebook.com/vijay.karthikeyan.7
Twitter handle: @vijaykarthikeyn
Instagram: @kvijayakarthikeyan

HEART QUAKE

K. VIJAYAKARTHIKEYAN

RUPA

Published by
Rupa Publications India Pvt. Ltd 2019
7/16, Ansari Road, Daryaganj
New Delhi 110002

Sales Centres:
Allahabad Bengaluru Chennai
Hyderabad Jaipur Kathmandu
Kolkata Mumbai

Copyright © K. Vijayakarthikeyan 2019

This is a work of fiction. Names, characters, places and incidents are either the
product of the author's imagination or are used fictitiously and any resemblance
to any actual person, living or dead, events or locales is entirely coincidental.

All rights reserved.
No part of this publication may be reproduced, transmitted,
or stored in a retrieval system, in any form or by any means,
electronic, mechanical, photocopying, recording or otherwise,
without the prior permission of the publisher.

ISBN: 978-93-5333-532-8

Third impression 2019

10 9 8 7 6 5 4 3

The moral right of the author has been asserted.

Printed at HT Media Ltd, Gr. Noida

This book is sold subject to the condition that it shall not,
by way of trade or otherwise, be lent, resold, hired out, or otherwise circulated,
without the publisher's prior consent, in any form of binding or
cover other than that in which it is published.

Contents

1. Running Away — 1
2. Face Off–Round 1 — 9
3. Face Off–Round 2 — 18
4. Heart Matters — 27
5. Lub Tub — 36
6. Number Games — 45
7. Fresh Trouble — 55
8. Tighter Knots — 65
9. Gathering Storm — 75
10. The Burst — 85
11. Trail Times — 95
12. Shocks, Storms, Breakthroughs — 105
13. Mask. Unmask. — 115
14. Unplotted — 125
15. Face Off–The Final — 135

Epilogue — 147

1

Running Away

It was a cold, rainy, dark October night. The Lal Bahadur Shastri National Academy of Administration stood like a colosseum in the heart of Mussoorie. LBSNAA, the abbreviated form of the academy, was the premier training institute for civil servants in the country. The Harry Potter fans among IAS probationers called it the 'Hogwarts' of Indian administration, whereas the X–Men fans called it the 'Xavier Institute' of India. Rakesh, however, felt he had landed in a 'jail'. Rakesh had never wanted this life, but his IAS father's desire to see his son as a bureaucrat was why he had ended up in LBSNAA. His dream was to be a stand-up comedian.

Rakesh had jumped over the Ganga gate of the academy and was running uphill towards the main road. He was escaping the academy. The rain had subsided by then, but Rakesh was still shivering as he gasped for air in a hypoxic state. He was struggling to walk with his heavy bag, and the slippery ground made it worse.

He was looking for a free ride to the Mall Road, but the stretch was completely deserted and silent. Rakesh had decided to walk to the taxi stand on the Mall Road from where he could escape to Delhi. He heard a car honk behind him. With a great sigh of relief, he turned around and signalled for a lift. His smile disappeared as the glass window of the car rolled down at the driver's seat. A face with the sharpest of eyes and the biggest of moustaches was smiling at him, showing an entire array of teeth. It was Vikram Kumar, or VK.

Vikram was about twenty-seven years old, born and brought up in Delhi. He was the tallest guy in most photos, the funniest guy at most parties, the mightiest guy in most physical activities and the craziest guy in most situations! He was street-smart and talked his way out of almost anything. Where his power of words failed, the power of his strong fists spoke! He took the IAS exam with the sole aim of getting into the system and changing it for the better.

'Don't try to stop me, VK! I'm going, and going for my own good!' said a desperate Rakesh.

'Okay, go! Who's stopping you? You were the one who stopped my car!'

'My mistake, I'm walking!'

'That was one of the most foolish and untimely ways of escape, by the way…considering the amount of fuss you have been making all over the academy!'

'Ya, laugh at me! What do you want now? Why are you even here?'

'Get into the car, it's cold. Let's go to Ganga Dhaba and talk. You may then leave,' said Vikram in a persuasive tone.

'I'm not going back to Ganga Dhaba or the Academy, ever!'

'Okay then, let's eat somewhere. I'm hungry. I will drop you anyplace you want after we eat. Let's go to Madhuban. Your favourite butter chicken will be available there.'

'FINE! But only for dinner!' Rakesh got into Vikram's car.

'This academy is a jail!' Rakesh kept repeating, as he devoured the butter chicken.

'I agree. I think it's like the *Bigg Boss* house,' Vikram said.

'Yeah. Actually, the jail inside the *Bigg Boss* house.'

'Okay. Why do you want to throw it all away?'

'Don't ask me again…as if you don't know!'

'You want to run away and become a stand-up comedian. This is a joke in itself—to make a living out of jokes!'

'Yeah, so what! My life itself is a joke,' Rakesh sounded extremely annoyed.

'Just that you are opting for a difficult route when there are easier ones!'

'Like what?'

'Listen to me, boss! If you leave the academy now, you will have to build your image from scratch. Who would want to watch a 'nobody'? But if you continue the training, you could become a Sub Collector or a Sub Divisional Magistrate (SDM) in a few months! This will become your USP for stand-up comedy. Tell me which new face would get more attention—an SDM's or a random aspiring stand-up comedian's?'

'A Sub Collector's!' there was a marked change in Rakesh's tone.

'There you go!'

'But, will I be able to manage both?'

'You are managing Reema and Neha. Can't you manage bureaucracy and comedy?'

'That was actually funny! *Chalo*, let's go back to the hostel!' By then Rakesh had had a complete change of mind.

Ten minutes later, Vikram and Rakesh sneaked into the hostel, chatting merrily.

'How do you do this every time...convince people?' Rakesh asked.

'Well, that's the primary job of a bureaucrat!' said Vikram, to which Rakesh nodded in agreement.

'That nod too! Combine this nod with persuasion and you have a good bureaucrat!' Vikram added. 'Combine that with bending the spine a bit will make "better" bureaucrats!'

'Ha ha!' Rakesh laughed.

Vikram and Rakesh tucked themselves into the comforts of their heated rooms and quilts.

'Oh man! Not again!' cried Vikram as the alarm went off at 5 a.m.

It seemed he had just got into bed, and it was morning already.

'Bunk PT! Try to get proxy,' Vikram told himself.

He got up, stretched a bit, wore his hooded-pullover, and started walking out of his room into the cold towards the polo ground.

It was a good ten-minute downhill walk from the hostel. The officer trainees—as the IAS probationers were called—were slowly crowding onto the road leading to the polo ground.

Shankar, the topper of their batch, was there already, flattering everyone with compliments and getting some in return. This meant the world to him. Shankar was obsessed with being the best at everything. Yet, he pretended that being a topper meant nothing to him.

Walking next to Shankar was Shamitha. She was the female version of Shankar, with a tinge of extra drama. Apart from gloating over glories in her UPSC exam, Shamitha's top to-do task was networking, although a major part of it involved portraying herself as the humblest person and the darling of the probationers.

As they walked towards the polo ground, Shankar proudly remembered how he had managed two marks more than Shamitha in General Studies, 3rd paper. Shamitha, meanwhile, assessed the behaviour of people that morning—those she wished, the way they responded and those who didn't.

Vikram was still looking at the two of them when someone clapped on his back. It was Rakesh.

'Thanks mate! What you told me last night was very insightful. It sounds dramatic now that I think about it; but I really thought that leaving this place was the only way out. Since I was forced into this, I thought the pressure of this job would strangle my passion. Last night, I realized that I could do both, and in fact, I would have an advantage by doing so!

'Hey! I wasn't getting sleep anyway. You have made a decision, and now, stand by it! Give your compliments to these two,' Vikram pointed at Shankar and Shamitha.

'Compliments for what? For the humblest drama ever?'

As his train moved towards Laxmipur, the screeching of wheels gave more impetus to Vikram's retrospection. He was fondly recollecting his days in the academy. He was to join as the Sub Collector/Sub Divisional Magistrate of Laxmipur the next day. It should have been one of the happiest days in his life, but it wasn't.

Anger, depression and sadness were choking Vikram. He looked pale. Unable to sleep, he tried to draw inspiration from his past to deal with the present. He felt exactly like Rakesh had felt the other day when he had tried to run away! Except, Vikram did not want to run away. He felt suffocated, frustrated and tied down for not being able to do what he wanted. His self-confidence was now broken, his sarcasm and sense of humour were gone. Yet, some force in him kept him going.

The train came to a screeching halt and the passengers were hurrying out.

Vikram slowly picked up his bag and started walking towards the door. His eyes had turned red due to lack of sleep. His heart was beating fast as he dawdled quietly towards the door. He saw fourteen to fifteen men, with bouquets and garlands, waiting to receive him at the platform.

'Namaste, SDM Saab!' they greeted him politely and started garlanding him.

A man stood behind Vikram. He readily collected the garlands and bouquets given to Vikram.

'He is your Dafedar Bahadur,' said a burly man in his late fifties, in a soft voice, 'my name is Ahmed and I am your PA, sir.'

The other officials introduced themselves to Vikram, and he shook hands with them.

Once the exchange of pleasantries was over, Vikram took his eyes off them for his first glimpse of Laxmipur. The first thing he noticed was a huge poster of a man. 'Rudra Pratap Rana, Home Minister' read the caption beneath the picture of a tall, bearded and well-built man in his late forties. The fake smile on his face and the darkened eyelashes evoked fear in any onlooker. Vikram's heart started beating faster now, as he stared at the picture. Vikram took a few deep breaths and slowly began to walk.

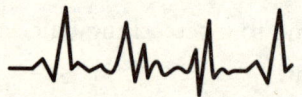

2

Face Off – Round I

'Why is there such a crowd? I know it is a Monday and people air their grievances. But why are there so many policemen, advocates and men in handcuffs?' enquired Vikram from the front seat of his jeep as the vehicle entered the office premises.

'This crowd is for the Law and Order Court, sir,' said Ahmed.

'Oh my god! These many people! Seriously?' Vikram couldn't believe his eyes.

'Yes, sir. There have been a lots of clashes, especially communal. Most of the SDM's time goes in sorting such issues on law and order and doing the Mantri's work, sir,' briefed Ahmed.

Vikram did not reply.

The Sub Divisional Magistrate's office was a small, old one built during the British times. The main door opened onto the SDM's chamber. On one side of the SDM's chamber was the courtroom cum meeting hall. It opened into the office section. Behind the office was an archives section, and the end of the building had the e-governance room with one computer, which had a Pentium III processor and a floppy disc drive.

'The computer room looks nice, much better than the SDM chamber,' remarked Vikram.

'You are right, sir. In fact, this computer room used to be the SDM's chamber. It was changed a few years ago.'

'Why?'

'There was a shootout and two people died right where you are standing, sir.'

Vikram hurriedly moved away from the spot. Not that there was something on the floor, which was covered with a carpet so old that it was waiting to be emancipated from the clutches of the building.

'What? Shootout? What was everyone doing? What did the SDM do?' Vikram couldn't believe what he had just heard.

'The shootout happened when the SDM was conducting his Monday court, sir! The court you are going to address today!' Bahadur couldn't resist commenting.

'Good timing, Dafedar!' Vikram, too, smiled and realized the situation he was about to face.

Vikram's phone rang. It was the District Magistrate Mahadev.

'Good morning, sir. I have just joined office. I was about to take an appointment and call on you.'

'No problem! You don't have to call on me; call Mantriji first. That is more important.'

Vikram did not respond to that. Instead, he told him about his plan of work.

'I will start with the Law and Order Court today, sir. Then, I will hear the public grievances. I have scheduled the hearing of land dispute cases for tomorrow.'

'No…no…no… These can wait. Mantriji's function in your division this weekend is your only priority. Focus on that and arrange for everything,' Vikram had a new agenda. A single point schedule!

'Okay, I will talk to you later,' Mahadev hung up.

Mahadev had been the Collector of Laxmipur for the past seven years—way beyond the regular tenure of any collector in the district. His secret to 'success' was simple—of RPR, by RPR, for RPR (Rudra Pratap Rana). He would blindly do whatever RPR asked of him, without caring about the consequences.

Vikram closed the door behind him and sat quietly in his chamber. He tried to focus on work but couldn't.

He was reminded of his time at the academy, but this time, the memories were disturbing.

'If it had not been for that event in LBSNAA,' he thought.

'Hi VK! Check your locker. You are the escort officer for the special guest Rudra Pratap Rana, a.k.a. RPR, the Home Minister of Uttar Pradesh, this weekend. It's an hour-long event; you can check with Mantriji's office and plan it accordingly,' said Rampal Singh, their course coordinator.

'Wow! That's a great opportunity for a troll fest!' laughed Rakesh. 'If I were you, I would have added a *Koffee with Karan* rapid fire round,' he continued.

'This is a wonderful opportunity to expose him,' remarked Jaidev, one of Vikram's close friends.

Jaidev Thackeray was an activist-turned bureaucrat from Maharashtra. He had radical ideas and extreme solutions for any situation. Vikram loved arguing with Jaidev, as their arguments brought out the best and most honest perspectives from them. Even though their opinions on various topics often differed, their goal remained the same—to change the system for good.

'Let me check with the Mantri's office if they agree to a "Q & A" with him. It will be better than listening to his boring speeches of self-praise,' said Vikram.

Vikram had worked as a journalist for a year for a popular political magazine in Delhi. Suddenly, the journalist in him had woken up, and he wanted to make this opportunity count.

Soon, the Mantri's office approved the Q & A session for the function. Vikram was also instructed to mail the questions that were to be asked during the session.

Vikram, Rakesh and Jaidev sat together, studying about RPR and drafted the questions.

Shamitha and Shankar, meanwhile, were setting their own agendas for the Mantri visit.

'Both of us are getting posted in the UP cadre anyway and have to spend the rest of our lives there. We will gather a group of colleagues, who are not being posted in UP, to meet the Mantri after the event. This will give us a head start in our career. It's always good to be in the good books of powerful political executives,' said Shamitha.

'Ya, ya,' Shankar agreed. 'We should talk to him nicely. This might help us get good postings once we are in UP,' he already knew the posts he would prefer.

Finally, the day arrived. Vikram wore a suit as per protocol. He knew that the spotlight would be on him that day. He also knew that he would have to face RPR many times during his postings in UP.

Vikram stood in front of the mirror and looked at the paper that had the questions. He took a few deep breaths and asked himself, 'Should I do this?'

'Yes, you should do this; isn't this the reason you are here in the first place?' the words echoed in his mind.

All the 160 probationers of the batch were formally attired and seated in the Sampoornanand Auditorium.

Members of the Press were not allowed, but Rakesh was ready with his phone to go live on Instagram from his account.

'This live webcast would get me thousands of followers on Instagram, which I would use for my stand-up comedies,' he laughed and told Vikram.

Jaidev was tense but was looking forward to the event. Shamitha and Shankar seated themselves prominently in the front row to be noticed by the Mantri.

'Hey Shamitha, you should meet the Mantri after the event,' suggested Indhu.

'No yaaa! These people have been asking me to do so, but I don't want to meet a politician,' shrugged Shamitha.

Shankar knew Shamitha too well. He asked, 'What will you tell Indhu when she sees you talking to Mantri?'

'That you people forced me to meet him!' she chuckled.

'Ladies and gentlemen, it's my proud privilege to welcome Shri Rudra Pratap Rana, the Home Minister of UP, to our academy today,' started Vikram as the Mantri got onto the dais.

The Mantri was a tall and brawny man, with a thick beard. He strode on the stage and addressed the crowd in his heavy and loud voice, 'Namaste.' He flashed his typical evil smile and took his seat.

Soon, the introduction was over. Vikram sat right opposite to RPR; the spotlights were on. Rakesh secretly went live on Instagram, and the Q & A session officially began.

Vikram: Sir, you are one of the most influential and powerful politicians in UP today. Everyone—the partymen, public, students—listen to you...

Shankar had already begun to feel insecure that about Vikram getting into the Mantri's good books and becoming a collector before him.

RPR was pleased and flashed his fake smile.

Vikram: ...but you have always misused your power, position and influence for your personal and political gains.

RPR's expression changed in a jiffy.

RPR: 'Hey! What do you think you are saying?! We had given you a list of questions to ask!'

Vikram: Sir, will you allow me to complete my question or are you scared? *Darr gaye?*

RPR: What? Scared? Me? Of a kid's question? Go on, ask!

By now, Rakesh's live feed had thousands of views and the news was spreading like wildfire. Popular television and YouTube channels had started sharing his feed.

Vikram: Sir, you have used the communal tension in your own district for your political gains; upscaled simple public issues into burning issues of the state only to increase your vote bank, the riots in 2006, 2009 and those last year... Last year, an entire village was burnt near Mirabad because of your inaction. The second issue against you is corruption... I can list out the others...

RPR got up from his seat and glared at Vikram. He

threw the mic away and walked towards him with long strides.

'Which party hired you to do this?' RPR and Vikram were standing up-close and looking angrily into each other's eyes. RPR almost took him by the collar, but somehow restrained himself. He was standing there like a raging bull, waiting to tear down anyone who came in its way. Vikram, too, stood like a soldier in a war field, facing the enemy. RPR's personal staff and security surrounded him, took him aside and gave him some water to drink. He threw the glass away.

Jaidev, who had become extremely emotional, suddenly started shouting, 'Rowdy Pratap Rana down down! Rowdy Pratap Rana down down!'

RPR looked away from Vikram and glared at Jaidev, as he was escorted by the minister's security.

The director and other senior officers of the academy tried to pacify the minister, took him to the office, and made arrangements to send him away peacefully.

Shankar and Shamitha had mixed emotions about the whole event. They were happy that Vikram's career was now screwed. They had one lesser competitor to contend with now. But they had lost their golden opportunity to get into the Mantri's good books.

Rakesh's video, meanwhile, was trending all over the country with a million real-time views. Hashtags such as #IASVsMantri and #AdhikariAgainstMantri were trending. #VikramKumar #Rakesh and #JaidevThackeray were trending too. Every news channel was telecasting the showdown between Vikram and RPR.

Shankar and Shamitha were now feeling extremely jealous that Vikram had become a superstar among the masses in an instance. They were also worried that if the Opposition party came to power, Vikram would get a posting ahead of batch toppers.

Vikram's heart was racing. He felt extremely uncomfortable, but deep inside, there was a sense of satisfaction. These were questions that people wanted to ask RPR. Vikram was a public servant; he got an opportunity to ask these questions and he took it. He didn't know if it was the right thing to do, but, surely felt right.

That was the first round between Vikram and RPR, and it was just the beginning...

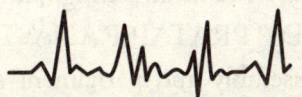

3

Face Off–Round 2

The footage from LBSNAA was the talk of the country. Memes and trolls about the event were flooding the Internet. There were raging debates across television channels. The Opposition parties took full cognizance of the situation and tried to exploit it to the hilt. There were posters of the confrontation and RPR intimidating Vikram, and banners that read 'ROWDY PRATAP RANA'. There were raging debates in the assembly and parliament sessions, and the party high command had summoned RPR for a detailed explanation.

Vikram became a national celebrity and was tagged as the 'Voice of the Common Man'. He switched off his phone, to avoid the constant phone calls, mails and messages. People waited for his version of the story.

Vikram asked the questions that the common man wanted to ask the Mantri, and there ended the story for him. He wasn't one bit interested in the media's attention and the drama that followed. He knew that the event would not end well, but he expected RPR to counter him word for word.

Meanwhile, inside the campus, he became the most unwanted soul, along with Jaidev and Rakesh. The three of them were straightaway suspended from the course and placed before an enquiry commission. Though some of their colleagues empathized with the trio, the remaining were of the opinion that what they did was extremely 'unofficer-like', and in the words of Rampal Singh, 'unbecoming of a civil servant'!

Shamitha and Shankar listed the trio's mistakes, suggesting ideas about how exactly an 'ideal' officer should behave under those circumstances to their friends at the academy. Each time they spoke about ideal officers, in groups, both Shamitha and Shankar secretly hoped that someone would name them. Whenever that happened, they would politely refuse the tag and make the fakest comments to validate their humility.

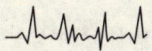

'Ohhh my god!' screamed Padma, Vikram's mother, as a six-and-a-half-foot-tall, bald man, weighing over 150 kg, took off their wall-mounted LCD television and threw it on the floor.

Padma's cry was so loud and filled with such despair

that it got the attention of their entire otherwise-quiet neighbourhood. Quite a few of their neighbours gathered outside their house. Gaurav, Vikram's father, ran into the living room. Padma stood in the middle of the room, helplessly crying and shouting at the men, who were randomly picking things up and breaking them. There were six of them—five tall and brawny men, with extreme thug-like looks, and a midget with an even more gangster-like appearance.

After recovering from the initial shock, Gaurav tried to fight one of them, but he was pushed down, kicked and beaten by the gang. Padma wailed as Gaurav bled from the cuts on his forehead, nose and ears. He was almost unconscious. By then, Padma too was lying on the floor, shell shocked and almost comatose.

'Who are you? What do you want? We are going to call the police,' the neighbours who had gathered outside confronted the goons.

They went straight to whoever questioned them, slapped and punched them in their stomachs and groins.

'You want to know the reason? Their son, the great Vikram Kumar IAS, one of the most corrupt officers you will see, has been bribed to start a smear campaign against our great leader. This is the punishment for indulging in corruption.'

As the goon continued to slander Vikram, someone struck him on his head from behind. The blow cracked open his skull and the blood gushed down his forehead. He almost blacked out but turned around and caught the person by the throat. He was surprised to see a woman, probably in her early thirties, grittily holding onto a broken window grill bar. Tears flowed down her cheeks as the man crushed her throat ruthlessly. Her grip on the grill bar loosened, and it fell from her grasp. The man went back a few steps and rammed her into the wall.

―――⌇⌇―――

'Do you even deserve to be called officers after what you have done, and the shame you have brought to the academy?' fired the director, who was also the chairman of the enquiry committee.

Vikram, Rakesh and Jaidev stood before the enquiry committee. Rakesh stood with folded hands, Jaidev held on to the side of the table, and Vikram had his hands tied behind him.

'You have misbehaved with an esteemed dignitary! Did you even think twice before blurting out those words? You were doing so well in training. All of us had high hopes from you!' the director told Vikram, who just stood motionless.

'And you! Shouting slogans like a goon on the street! Is that why you cleared the civil service exam?' the director spoke to Jaidev now.

'Sir, he is a rogue. He got what he deserved!'

'And what are you? A thorough gentleman? Is that how

you behaved?'

The director shut Jaidev up with a volley of questions.

'And here is our official broadcaster! We should have let you run away that night. Do you fools think we are unaware of your activities? Why don't you make a stand-up comedy on your own life?' he mocked Rakesh.

'All three of you are going to lose your jobs now. Happy? The job for which you worked night and day…gone! Just because of one moment of madness! Fools!'

'Is there anything you wish to say before the committee?'

'I would still stand by what I did, sir. I never misbehaved. I was polite with him throughout the session. As a public servant, I just wanted to ask him what the public really would have, if they had the opportunity. When offenders and their deeds are questioned, they give rise to insecurity and fear. This insecurity and fear make people reduce, if not stop, the wrongdoings they are being questioned for,' replied Vikram.

'See, you just called the Mantri an offender. Though your intentions are good, you are overstepping the line. I have nothing more to say. Your dismissal orders will be issued in a few days. All of you can leave now!' the director concluded.

The three of them quietly left the room.

'I studied medicine for the sake of my mother, became an IAS officer because my father asked me to. All I wanted was to be a stand-up comedian! Leaving the academy is not a problem, but doing so with a bad reputation will get me nothing. And how will I face my father? My head is reeling,' Rakesh was in tears.

'This place, this system... It's all so unfair. I'm not accountable to anyone, and I don't care about my reputation. Let them chuck me out. I'm waiting!' Jaidev roared angrily and punched the wall.

'Even this punch will be added to your charge sheet. They are watching us,' added Vikram when his phone rang.

After the initial 'hello' and a few 'hmms', Vikram was just holding the phone. Rakesh noticed that his expression was brave, but his hand trembled.

Rakesh couldn't believe the ever-confident and composed Vikram was reacting that way.

Vikram broke down after he hung up the phone and sat on the floor, crying out, with his head in his hands.

Rakesh and Jaidev put their arms around him and tried to comfort him.

'That scoundrel sent his men to my house,' Vikram cleared his throat as he spoke.

'Oh! I knew that rascal would do something like that,' Jaidev's anger knew no bounds.

'Both my parents are injured and hospitalized. My sister Swetha...' he paused and cried.

'My sister Swetha was rammed into the wall. She is in the ICU now. The baby she was carrying had to be aborted.'

Rakesh, too, began to cry. Jaidev kicked the floor so hard that the tiles came off.

Just then, a man in a safari suit, wearing dark shades, entered the room and handed a phone to Vikram.

Vikram took the phone in an indescribable state of mental agony. He didn't even have the mind or strength to say hello.

The voice at the other end laughed out loud for about half a minute. By now, Vikram knew who it was.

'National hero! How are you? Why are you crying like a baby? You are supposed to be a powerful officer taking on the baddies. Yes, I'm a rowdy and a baddie. What will you do now? You can do nothing! You people think too much about those three letters—IAS—behind your name, no? Let me show you that those three letters are nothing!' RPR was still fuming. Vikram could feel the heat in his voice.

RPR continued, 'You know what? You will not lose your job. In fact, I'm just gonna do the opposite. I will have you posted in my district! Do you know the greatest form of humiliation? It's seeing how powerful your enemy is day in and day out and realizing your impotence to go against him. That feeling is the greatest humiliation. That is worse than death. You will feel it every single day. And the same goes for your friends.'

That was the second face off between RPR and Vikram.

The very thought of that day made Vikram sweat profusely.

It was only an hour since he had joined as the SDM of Laxmipur, but he couldn't take his mind off the things that had brought him there.

There was a knock at the door and Ahmed came in running.

'Sir! Sir! The entire media is here! Not just the *localwala*, but those from Lucknow and Delhi, too, have arrived. About a hundred of them have gathered outside, sir. They are also showing a video of you standing face-to-face with our Mantri, sir! Even our DM stands with folded hands in front of him. We don't know what's happening, and we are scared, sir,' said Ahmed in an extremely panicky tone.

'Don't worry, I will take care if it!' assured Vikram.

He walked towards the door to address the media. Every incident that had occurred during the two face-offs ran through his mind. Every cry of his family and every word spoken by RPR echoed in his ears.

He opened the door slowly and walked towards the mics, with cameras flashing all around him.

'Sir, we couldn't contact you after that sensational interview with the Mantri. How does it feel to become a national hero overnight?'

'How do you feel now?'

'How will you work with the same Mantri now?'

'Are you planning for a transfer?'

'Did the Opposition actually bribe you to ask those questions?'

Some fifty questions were asked in less than a minute.

After about ten minutes of questioning and being unable to elicit a response from Vikram, the media went quiet.

Vikram started to speak in a low tone, 'What has happened has happened. I have a job to do now. I hope to fulfil my duties to the best of my abilities.'

'What about your relationship with Mantriji?'

'The same relationship any official has with a minister. I will work with our Mantriji and ensure peace and development of Laxmipur,' said Vikram calmly.

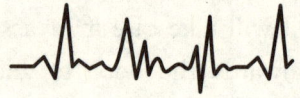

4

Heart Matters

It was a cold, foggy morning in Laxmipur, and the roads were barely visible. Vikram had stepped out for his routine jog. He could just about see the people near him. The thick fog hid even the giant-sized banners and posters of RPR. Vikram briefly stopped at Kothi Khas Bagh palace, clicked some pictures and continued to jog. By now, the sunrays had begun to show. Suddenly, Vikram realized that there were more RPR banners on the route he was on. The banners and posters were all over the place, and he noticed a huge gate made of grills at the corner of the road. The nameplate of the building read 'Rudra Pratap Rana, Home Minister'. There were a few cops near the gate and the sound of the police walkie talkie was distinctly audible. The house seemed like a fort surrounded by a concrete wall, half of which was covered with hundreds of RPR banners.

'A house full of scarecrow boards,' Vikram laughed and

continued running. Just as he was about to cross the house, the gates opened. Vikram thought that the moment he had been dreading had arrived. He briefly paused, expecting RPR to walk out wearing makeup.

He heard a bark and saw a woman, in her early thirties, come out of the house with a yellow Labrador. She was almost as tall as Vikram, and had her hair tied up. She had a distinctly pointed nose and long limbs. She wore a pink sleeveless t-shirt and red track pants, which matched her red shoes. She noticed Vikram looking at her and recognized him instantly.

'Oh my god! She must be a woman from that guy's family,' Vikram murmured to himself, took his eyes off her and resumed jogging.

'Hi! You are Vikram Kumar IAS aren't you?' she called out.

'Yeah,' murmured Vikram, turning only halfway towards her.

She too started running alongside Vikram.

'I have heard stories about you!' she said.

'Oh, is that so? Nice!' Vikram didn't know what to say. He smiled sheepishly and continued jogging.

'You see that temple there?' she asked.

'Ya.'

'RPR killed two people right in front of it twenty years ago. He chopped the arms off one of them before killing him. All because they wrote an exposè on him in a local magazine!'

Vikram was aghast imagining himself mutilated. The woman started laughing seeing Vikram's expression.

They then quietly jogged for some time.

'You see those hamlets near that lake? Ten years ago, RPR burnt that entire stretch just because a few people from the village messed with him. He usually doesn't spare anyone who messes with him. He waits years for his revenge,' she said and started to laugh, as Vikram's face turned pale.

They soon came across a burial ground.

'So, are you going to tell me that half the people buried here were killed by RPR, and some of them were even buried alive?' Vikram taunted the woman.

'Actually yes!' she burst into laughter—so loud that people paused to look at her; and her dog Timmy, who was running along with them, started barking.

Ideally, Vikram should have picked up a fight with her, but he didn't. Despite her taunts, something about her attracted Vikram. Perhaps it was the way she teased him.

Vikram had never had a girlfriend. He had had a few close friends who were girls, but no 'girlfriends'! Even though he thought he liked this woman, the fact that she belonged to RPR's family was a huge deterrent for him to even consider getting involved. He didn't even ask her name. But he felt that she was a nice person.

He stood there thinking about these things.

'Politicians are either a tease or they boss around or take people for granted,' Vikram commented.

'Ya, ya! They are all the same,' she replied, just about controlling her laughter.

'Not just the politicians, their families, too, are very arrogant!' Vikram continued.

'Not always though!' she replied.

'Anyway, I'll make a move. Have a lot of work. Good day to you!' said Vikram and started jogging towards his house.

'Good day to you too, and take care of your arms and legs…and that tongue too!' she shouted before heading home.

Ever since Vikram joined as the SDM of Laxmipur, he was experiencing a continuous pain on the left side of his chest.

'Could be a heart problem,' suggested Bahadur when he heard about it.

'Why does everyone want me dead today? I simply don't understand!'

'Who else told you so, sir?' asked Bahadur anxiously.

'Forget it! Take me to the best doctor in town once we are done for the day,' said an annoyed Vikram.

Vikram visited the city group's Blue Line Hospital for his check-up. Bahadur ran in front of Vikram to open the door for him. Vikram heard a familiar laughter as he entered the room.

'Hi! Please have a seat. Dr Veda Agarwal, consultant

cardiologist,' she stretched out her arm to shake hands with him.

'Vikram Kumar!' he said with a firm handshake.

'How many times do you need an introduction? You didn't even ask my name this morning!' said Veda.

'Sorry about that! Also, I didn't know you were a doctor.'

'Why? Do you only ask doctors their names?'

'No, no, it's not like that!'

'So what brings you to a cardiologist? You seemed fine this morning. Did my stories of RPR scare you?'

Somehow, the more Veda teased Vikram, the more he liked her.

She started examining him after discussing his physical ailments.

'Unbutton your shirt. Let's see what or who is in your heart,' she said as she picked up her stethoscope.

Vikram, slightly abashed, unbuttoned his shirt, as Veda quickly examined him.

'Nothing to worry. It is a muscle strain, seemingly from a new workout routine,' she said.

'I'll prescribe a muscle relaxant and a couple of medicines; should be okay in a week's time,' she continued.

'Can I run until then?'

'Yes, you can! Avoid upper body exercises and lifting weights. Running won't be a problem. Especially if you are running with a cardiologist and her dog; it shouldn't be a problem at all!'

'Can I ask you something?'

'Ya, go ahead.'

'How are you related to RPR?'

'How am I related to RPR? He is the MLA of my constituency; he happens to live in the same locality as I do, and most importantly, his mother is bedridden, and I attend to her at his house. For a hefty fee though! These are the only ways RPR and I are related,' said Veda with a big smile.

'So you checked on his mom this morning, and that's when we met, on your way out,' concluded a relieved Vikram.

'There you go! You thought I was having an affair with RPR, didn't you?' she burst out laughing.

'No! Frankly, no. Never thought about it to that extent. I thought you might be his sister or something!'

'His photographs are all over the city, right? You distinctly remember that face, right? And yet, you thought I was his sister?'

This time Vikram burst into laughter.

'Finally, I have made you laugh. I noticed how tense you were this morning and tried to lighten the mood! I have been following you since the Q & A video was released. I thought no one had the guts to question him. I truly admire you for that! I tease only those whom I like.'

'Nice! Anyway, in the interest of my health, as you suggested, I don't mind running with a cardiologist in the mornings.'

'And her dog too! What did Timmy ever do to you!'

'Ha ha!'

'See you tomorrow morning then. I have prescribed a scan; please get it done before leaving. I'll share the results with you soon. So, in the interest of your heart and its well-being, you must share your number with me.'

Vikram and Veda exchanged numbers, and he got up to leave.

Veda called for the nurse.

'Sister, please take sir to the echo room right away and get the scan done. I'll call and inform the radiologist.'

'The echo room is full with emergency cases, ma'am. There has been a sudden inflow of patients, ma'am.'

'I don't mind waiting to get the scan done. See you tomorrow morning with Timmy! Bye!'

'Bye.'

Veda liked Vikram when she saw him in the LBSNAA video for the first time. Both of them realized that they got along pretty well, and they looked forward to their morning jogs.

―⁓⁓⁓―

Deafening drumbeats and the sounds of unending crackers set the tone for the Vikram–RPR meeting. RPR got out of his car in slow motion as his supporters ran towards him with garlands.

Mahadev ran in front of the supporters to open the door of the car for the minister and be the first one to garland him. RPR greeted Mahadev with an ear-to-ear grin, and then met his party's men with his typical fake smile. He walked towards the stage, where Vikram was standing. The drumbeats rose to a crescendo as RPR approached Vikram. Both of them exchanged cordial namastes and RPR quickly got onto the stage.

RPR called for Mahadev.

'Have you done as I had asked?' enquired RPR.

'Yes, sir! All pending public grievances and applications have been processed, but we haven't issued the grants to the public, sir. The public thinks the files are still pending, sir. Thus, we have kept all applications *ready, yet pending*, sir.'

'Ready, yet pending! Waaaah! Only you can make such things happen, Mahadev.'

Mahadev's day was made with RPR's comment. He couldn't hide his happiness, yet continued to showcase his administrative skills to RPR.

'Many from the crowd will approach you, complaining about their subdivisions, pensions and certificates, sir. You may order me to address these concerns immediately. We will pretend that we have acted on them as per your order, sir. You may then issue the grants on this stage itself, sir. All of this is your idea, sir. I'm just the implementer,' said Mahadev humbly.

'Okay, okay, get along with the proceedings. This is one

of the ways to keep my vote bank swelling,' said RPR.

'This is one of the ways how I get to keep the same post for so many years and my bank balance swelling,' Mahadev thought happily.

Soon, the drama took place and the event gradually ended. RPR was heading toward his car. As he crossed Vikram, he stopped for a moment.

'Did you see the crowd?'

'Yes, sir.'

'That is just a small sample of my strength. See how your DM works for me, and learn from such people. Realize your worth as you work for me and keep reflecting on this self-worth throughout your tenure here. You will helplessly stand in front on me and work for me, for as long as I wish! This is your fate! Enjoy it!'

Vikram smiled.

'Why are you smiling?'

'Nothing, sir, just wanted to ask when your next programme is scheduled here.'

'Mahadev will tell you! In the meantime, continue your helpless, impotent existence!'

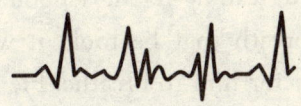

5
Lub Tub

Kiran Kumar had been driving the City International school bus for the past seven years. He has always been an active man. He enjoyed picking up the children from their bus stops. Even though the conductor and his assistant were always on board the bus, he would willingly help parents carry the school and lunch bags. At times, the thirty year old would playfully lift the kids and carry them to their seats.

It was yet another day for Kiran, but an uneasy feeling had been bothering him since morning. He had picked up all the kids from the bus stops and had been driving on the Arts College Road, leading to the school.

With every breath that he took, it was getting more and more difficult for him to breathe. He felt his chest get tighter and tighter, and a sharp pain was radiating from his pericardial region. Kiran was losing control of not only himself but also of the steering wheel. The bus was swaying from side to side on the road and his vision was getting blurry. His assistant noticed Kiran's slumping body and rushed to take control of the wheel.

By then, Kiran was unconscious and blood was oozing out of his nose. Only the white sclera of the eye was visible; the iris and pupil had completely disappeared.

Pawan Garg was one of the most flourishing auditors in town. He got married in his late forties and had two kids. Though he was working for some of the major businessmen in the city, he always maintained a low profile and led a simple life.

That day, it was office as usual at 7 a.m. for Pawan. He was working out the taxable income details of a client, chewing pan and browsing through the sheets.

Suddenly, he felt an excruciating pain on the left side of his chest. It was as if someone was stabbing him with daggers. It was so painful that tears flowed down his cheeks.

He felt suffocated with every passing second, and it seemed a matter seconds before he would pass out.

Despite the unbearable pain, Pawan tried to stay conscious as long as possible, but he was horrified to see blood streaming down his eyes instead of tears.

THUD!

He fell on the table, crippled with pain and fear.

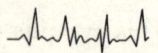

Kiran's assistant finally stopped the school bus. Everyone in the bus ran towards Kiran.

'Call the ambulance,' a kid shouted. Some of the kids had started crying by then.

Kiran's assistant looked around and searched frantically for his phone, which had fallen from his pocket amidst the commotion. The clock was ticking, and Kiran's assistant still couldn't find it. The conductor did not own a phone and the kids too didn't have phones. Kiran was lying motionless on the floor of the bus. It was difficult to make out if he was breathing at all.

Suddenly, a small girl, around seven or eight years of age, stepped forward and walked towards Kiran. She put her hands into Kiran's pocket and pulled out his phone. She quickly gave it to Kiran's assistant who dialled the emergency number. The call went to the police control room, which was redirected to emergency medical services.

'We will send the ambulance immediately. By the fastest route, we will take twenty minutes to reach you. But the prognosis looks grave,' said the voice on the other end.

Pawan lay motionless in his own pool of blood on the floor. No one knew the state he was in. Incidentally, the *chaiwala* walked into the room and was shocked by what he saw in front of him. Having seen Pawan for years, he was disturbed and desperately shook him to wake him up. He held his hands and tried to pull him up but couldn't.

The air-conditioner in the room had been running continuously and Pawan's hands had turned cold. Unable to lift him, the *chaiwala* cried loudly and ran out for help. Others in the office arrived and drove him to the hospital.

'I can't feel his pulse,' remarked one of Pawan's friends who was holding him, as the car sped toward the hospital.

'*To become a successful politician, you need to be a good actor.*

To become a successful actor, you need to be a good politician.

To become a successful bureaucrat though, you need to be both!'

Rakesh said with his impeccable timing, and the crowd responded with a thunderous applause.

'Wow! This guy is not just funny, but quite smart too!' remarked Veda, sipping her glass of amla juice.

Vikram and Veda were sitting in one of the municipal corporation's parks after their jog and were watching Rakesh's stand-up comedy performances on Vikram's phone.

'Yeah! You cannot just label him as a stand-up comedian.

His acts are quite thought-provoking. This makes him different from the others. He has become extremely popular and the tickets to his shows sell out quickly. He performed here last week—just a few days before I arrived at Laxmipur. It's a pity that I missed his show. Would you like to join me for his next show, if he performs somewhere close by?' said Vikram expectantly.

'Ya, sure! Imagine him ridiculing RPR in this city!' Veda laughed.

'Well, I had tried a similar stint last year, and he had broadcasted it to the whole world. We all know how that went.' Vikram laughed.

'It's so nice to see you laugh like that—natural and from the heart. I really like it!' said Vikram.

'I like it when you laugh as well!' blushed Veda.

'Wow! I have never seen you blush!' Vikram pointed out.

'I *did not* blush. Have you seen girls blush?'

'Of course, I have.'

'Have you only seen them blush or…' teased Veda.

'Hello Doctor Heart! My heart is still untouched, okay?'

Veda smiled, and with every response of Vikram's, she blushed a little more.

'Do you know what boys mean when they say they don't have a girlfriend?' asked Vikram.

'Yeah! It means they would like to date, isn't it?' she chuckled.

Vikram nodded and said, 'So, you will answer with

another question. There is another angle to it. It is also because they want to know if the girl is interested in the guy.'

'Oh! Boys' psychology, huh? The boy could directly ask her about her status, na? What's with these tricks?'

'What about you then?' Vikram took a shot at her.

'Well! I was in a relationship when I was in college... with a Punjabi boy.'

'And?' asked Vikram.

'He got married,' Veda sighed.

'That's it?'

'Yes, a four-worded sad love story—My boyfriend got married!'

'Then?'

'He must have kids by now. What do I know? I don't stalk my ex-boyfriend!'

'I asked about you?' clarified Vikram.

'I did stalk him for a few months,' she scoffed, 'then, I moved on to pursue post-graduation and got on with life. Haven't found anyone as interesting yet.'

'You should rather say that you haven't found a guy interesting enough! Every guy is interesting!' Vikram asserted.

'Hmm...' Veda seemed at a loss for words.

'So, are you single now?'

'Of course I'm single now. Why else would I be sitting under this tree in an ill-maintained municipal park, sipping amla juice with you?'

Then Veda's phone rang. There was a drastic change of

expression on her face as she spoke.

'Have to go to the hospital immediately,' said Veda, getting up and putting down her glass of juice.

'Will call you asap! Sorry for running away!' she said and started walking briskly towards the park's exit.

'"And then, she left"—my four-worded sad story!' shouted Vikram.

'I will tell you more! Will call you in an hour! Bye!' she shouted back.

―⌇⌇―

'Both the patients are critical, ma'am!' said the nurse, as Veda walked into the emergency room. The chief, the cardiothoracic surgeon, the on-duty anaesthetist and a few junior doctors had already assembled.

'It's too late and too risky to go for a surgery now,' the cardiothoracic surgeon observed, taking stock of the situation.

Pawan was lying motionless on the bed. His heart rate had been steadily falling, and they were losing him.

The chief doctor, Fawad Khan, was giving out instructions to Veda and her colleagues. They began the treatment immediately, giving him injection shots at regular intervals and monitoring every change in Pawan's body.

Pawan's kids—his ten-year-old daughter and seven-year-old son—and his wife were waiting impatiently outside the emergency room (ER). His daughter, Ria, was trying to peep into the ER to catch a glimpse of her father every time its door opened. Her eyes were brimming with tears as she looked around anxiously, trying to make sense of the situation. All she wanted in life at that moment was to save her father. She stood right in front of the door, with folded hands, praying with all her might for her father's recovery. Her mother and brother sat near a Ganapathy idol and wept bitterly.

Soon, the door opened and Veda walked out. She walked up to Ria, placed her hands on her head and said, 'Your papa will be with you soon! He loves you so much that he refused to leave. You will be able to talk to him soon.'

'Your smile is the most beautiful thing I have ever seen,' continued Veda, as Ria smiled and wiped her tears.

They were shifting Pawan from the emergency room to the ICU, where he was to be monitored. He was out of danger, but he was still a long way from recovery.

'Great work, doctor!' congratulated the nurse.

'Good that we could at least save this one. Really sad that we couldn't save the other patient!' said Veda.

'Seven such cases have come in since last night, ma'am! Each one of them had ailments related to the heart. Two of them have died. Something seems wrong, ma'am!' the nurse said in a worried tone.

Veda was suddenly reminded of Vikram. It was more than an hour since she had left him, and he was the first person who came to her mind after the proceedings of the day.

'Hi! There were two emergency cases with heart-related ailments. We tried our best and saved one, but we couldn't save the other. About seven such cases have come in since last night, and we have lost two out of them. I see a worrisome pattern here!' Veda told Vikram.

'Please switch on the TV and see the news,' said Vikram.

Veda clawed at the remote control and switched on the TV.

'Mysterious heart disease strikes Laxmipur! Death toll rises to 104 in less than 24 hours! Fear, confusion and panic all over Laxmipur!' Every news channel flashed the breaking news; the reporters were having a field day, and the visuals were extremely disturbing.

'How many more will die? What is this mysterious heart disease? And more importantly, who is next?' shouted the anchor at the top of his voice.

'What the f###!' Veda couldn't believe what she was seeing.

There was a knock on her door and the nurse came in running.

'Ma'am, five similar cases have been brought to the emergency room; three of them are bleeding through their eyes and one patient has been declared dead already.'

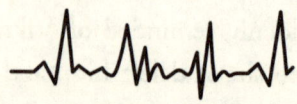

6

Number Games

'What is the health department doing? What action has been taken?' RPR was fuming, and shouted at the top of his voice.

RPR and the health minister, Manoj Kumar, had jointly called for an emergency meeting with the concerned officials to assess the situation in Laxmipur.

The sensational news about the mysterious heart disease claiming lives and causing substantial morbidity rapidly as an 'outbreak' was sending shivers across the entire state. Everyone was completely baffled by the situation and before they could even blink, more than a hundred lives were lost! The entire administrative machinery still did not know what was to be done. The healthcare machinery was treating the symptoms conservatively, stabilizing and saving as many people as possible, but no one could get to the root of the matter. Not even close!

'How can an outbreak of heart attacks happen? It's not diarrhoea or cholera! We are talking about heart attacks! A sudden outbreak of bloody heart attacks! People are bleeding from their eyes! Can anyone comprehend anything?' asked Manoj Kumar in an extremely frustrated tone.

No one in the meeting hall, including Vikram, knew what exactly was happening. People looked at each other, pretended not to look at one other and avoided eye contact with the two ministers; some were scared and began to pray; Vikram was thinking of ways to contain the situation, and then there was Mahadev—the district magistrate chewing his cashew nuts slowly and burping on the sidelines.

'The dean of the medical college and the chairman of Super Global Hospitals are now in discussion with some senior doctors for arriving at the cause and deriving the protocols of the treatment, sir,' said the deputy director of health services, politely standing up.

'Put the dean on the line immediately, Mahadev ji,' said RPR.

Mahadev's peaceful cashew nut feast was interrupted, and he suddenly exhibited his agility and 'activeness' in taking orders to address the issue. He called out to his personal clerk, who carried out 90 per cent of Mahadev's work, for his phone. The remaining 10 per cent of the work was usually not done!

Mahadev got hold of the phone, but despite his best effort to be quick, was painfully slow even in looking up the dean's number and then dialling it!

'Seems like DM Saab doesn't even dial the numbers of people he wants to call. Even that is done by his PC,' RPR mocked.

Mahadev displayed a ridiculously embarrassing smile and somehow got the dean on the line.

'Dean Saab, what is the progress? Have you found out anything?' asked RPR.

'No, sir! We are working on it!' replied the dean.

'Working on it? You are working on what—building another Taj Mahal? Don't give me such *sarkari* replies! I need a solution in 24 hours! DM Saab, disconnect the call!' said RPR.

Mahadev promptly disconnected the call without even waiting for the dean's response.

'Look! We do not want your replies; we want a solution! Understand?' RPR's loud voice was reverberating in the hall.

'SDM Saab, got it?' RPR singled out Vikram.

'Yes, sir,' Vikram nodded. Mahadev, too, nodded involuntarily, as he was so used to nodding.

'Anybody can ask sensational questions and create drama; an IAS officer is respected because he or she has the ability to think and take clear decisions for the benefit of the society. If you are really that, then act like one!' RPR continued.

'Will do my best, sir,' assured Vikram.

The General Hospital of Laxmipur was the busiest place in the town these days, as the disease was at its virulent best. Media vans were stationed all around the hospital and live commentary over treatments, death reports and post mortems were transmitted as breaking news even without verification. It was all happening at Laxmipur General Hospital.

Kiran woke up slowly on a bed in the corner of the ICU. He opened his eyes and slowly gathered consciousness. He had no one waiting for him outside the ICU. No family or friends. All he had were the wishes of a few of his colleagues and unconditional love of the school children with whom he interacted daily.

'Inform our school chairman that I am alive, doctor,' was the first thing that Kiran said. Having been left with no family, it was his school chairman who had brought him up and had given him whatever he had in life. Kiran vouched utmost love and loyalty to the chairman and his family. Kiran tried to get up slowly but a nurse came running in and asked him to lie down.

Meanwhile, Sameer Gupta, the Opposition party leader of Laxmipur, was at the GH, taking stock of the situation, speaking to the doctors, and doing rounds of the wards though he wasn't let into the ICU. He came out with a scathing attack on RPR and the ruling government for failing to tackle such a massive public health issue.

'The ruling party's lack of empathy for the poor, lack

of people-centric policies, price rise and a fascist attitude are causing these heart problems. If Mantriji, the CM and the government step down, people will be free from such ailments. Shall we give it a go? As long as this party is in power, and this RPR is in power, people will continue to suffer!'

'Sir, did you realize that you just cursed your own people?' asked a reporter.

'How did I curse my people?'

'You just did, and it is on record.'

'I just said that this irresponsible government, the CM and RPR are the root cause of this issue and so many other issues!'

'So are you telling us that this government is responsible for this?'

'Yes, of course! Time will prove me right!'

Vikram, meanwhile, quickly visited the hospitals in the city and called for a meeting in his own office.

'This is what these *sarkari* people do whenever there is an issue—call for meetings!' murmured a doctor to his friend, as they stepped into Vikram's chamber.

'Arrey, don't crib, yaar! We will eat the samosas and kachoris and go back to our duties,' remarked his friend, as they took their seats in the last row.

'See, this is not like your routine meetings. I know all of us have a task, and not much time left. So let me get straight to the point. What is causing these peculiar heart attacks? Any sure-shot causatives found?'

'No, sir,' said everyone in unison.

'How many patients have been affected so far?'

'About 2,000 people, sir,' said the dean.

'What are the common signs and symptoms among the affected people?'

'Excruciating pain in the pericardial region, acute respiratory distress...'

'I am an arts graduate. Can you please talk in a layman's language?' Vikram interrupted.

'Yes, sir. Sudden, severe pain on the left side of the chest, sudden difficulty in breathing, bleeding tendencies, especially from the eyes and the ears, have been found, sir,' said the dean

'What's your observation from this?'

'Though there are four to five common symptoms among the affected patients, the intensity of the disease is varying across the affected population. We do not know the exact reason, but one thing that is clear is that the disease doesn't treat everyone the same way,' replied the dean.

'Hope you have done a complete analysis based on the patients' profiles?' asked Vikram.

'Yes, sir. We have broken down the numbers based on the patients' characteristics. We have a PowerPoint presentation ready, sir,' replied the dean.

'No PowerPoint please. Most of the time, we think that our job is done once our PowerPoint presentation is done! Just give me the numbers as I asked for,' Vikram said in a sharp tone.

'Is there any particular age group that is affected?'

'No, sir, but none of the children have been affected so far. The youngest person to be affected is seventeen years old. The disease has been mapped between seventeen and seventy, sir.'

'Does it peak somewhere?'

'Doesn't peak, sir, there is a gradual increase though, from about thirty-two and sixty-two.'

'Our people have the tendency to book every other heart ailment into this, especially among the older age groups. And, once the government announces compensation for the affected families, I don't want these numbers to swell up. Let me be clear on this!'

'Yes, sir.'

'What about the sex ratio that is affected?'

'Clearly, more men are affected, sir. Although about 15 per cent of the total affected population are women.'

'Does this show any strong correlation?'

'Not much, sir, as most diseases have a strong male preponderance. This is slightly unusual, but we don't have enough evidence yet to establish a strong correlation.

'Has it affected only a particular class of people?'

'We don't have the exact details, sir, but having seen more

than a hundred patients personally, I don't think there is only a particular class that is affected, sir. I have seen bankers, I have seen businessmen, I have seen drivers, office peons… all of them are affected, sir.'

'Have you established the treatment protocol?'

'Yes, sir. We have clearly worked out certain conservative treatment methodologies, which can be applied uniformly and prove to be truly lifesaving!'

'Good. I want all the hospital heads present here to take note of the common treatment protocol and follow that uniformly. Any deviations from that will be strictly dealt with!' Vikram gave out stern instructions.

'The public relations officer is to convey the highlights of this meeting to the press, and doctors are to start acting quickly as per the protocol. The dean is to also form a separate team of interested and spirited doctors to identify the cause as early as possible,' he concluded.

Just as everyone was leaving, Vikram called out to the dean, 'Doctor, have we checked out the localities from where the cases have come so far?'

'No, we usually do that only for communicable, especially vector-borne diseases, sir'.

'Can we please do that for this too?'

'Yes, sir. Will check and revert,' said the dean.

Veda walked in as the dean was leaving the room.

'So? What's happening?' asked Vikram.

'You just had a meeting; you tell me,' replied Veda.

'Nothing is clear yet,' said Vikram.

'This is what everyone has been saying,' Veda replied.

Veda took out the glass of water, kept it on the table for Vikram and drank from it.

'Do you want another glass?'

'No, no, this is fine. I was thirsty,' said Veda, not revealing that she purposefully drank from Vikram's glass, making a childish gesture.

'Would you like to have coffee?'

'No coffee! Do you have amla juice?'

'You have to wait until morning for that.'

'Or should I ask someone to get it now? From our park?' said Vikram as an afterthought.

Vikram's mind was completely occupied with the disease. A lot of questions were on his mind. He wanted to talk to Veda in a more relaxed, cheerful frame of mind, but he could not.

'Aren't you bothered by these things?' he asked Veda.

'Of course, I am! What do you think?'

'But you don't seem to show it.'

'Hello! I'm a doctor! I see so many patients every day. I'm so used to the routine. I'm fully involved with the case in the hospital; once I'm out, I take it off my mind! That's a doctor's life,' she smiled.

Vikram's phone rang. It was the dean. It was the call he had been waiting for.

'You were right, sir. We compared the localities of the

affected people, and 75 per cent of the people belong to the other side of the river and 35 percent of the people belong to one area—MN Nagar! I have also mailed you the map, sir,' said the dean.

Vikram opened the mail and found the map. It was marked with red spots on the western side of the river Chamara, and the right edge of the city had the most number of red spots, which corresponded to MN Nagar!

'Oh my god!' gasped Vikram.

7

Fresh Trouble

Vikram suddenly woke up when the doorbell rang a couple of times. He got up slowly and pulled out his phone from under his pillow; it was about 6 a.m. in the morning. There were about fifteen missed calls. Rubbing his eyes, he got up from his bed and walked towards the front door.

It was the Deputy Superintendent of Police, Raghuveer, standing at the front door. Almost as tall as Vikram, slightly more muscular than him, bearded, with a big moustache, Raghu was just into his thirties. He had been eagerly awaiting Vikram. He did the customary salute to Vikram and went straight to the point.

'About fifty people are protesting in front of the Everest Chemical Factory, sir.'

'Why suddenly a protest there?'

'There have been reports circulating in the media that the current heart attack catastrophe in Laxmipur is due to a poisonous gas leak from the chemical factory. These people are protesting outside the factory to have it shut down!'

'Is this is based only on media reports, or is there any concrete evidence?'

'Not sure about the evidence, sir, but the news is making headlines in the media. A powerful activist from Maharashtra has already joined the protestors,' said Raghu.

'You can proceed to the spot and take care of the routine crowd control activities; I'll visit the place in a while, depending on the situation.'

'Yes, sir,' said Raghu, and proceeded to the spot.

Vikram then called PA Ahmed. 'Ask all our revenue staff in and around MN Nagar area to do a household level survey about any abnormal odour; if they have had any breathing distresses in the last three days; tabulate the data household-wise and submit the reports by noon.

'Yes, sir,' replied Ahmed.

Vikram then called the dean. 'Doctor, kindly backtrack all respiratory and cardiac cases in the last three days to MN Nagar and see how many are from MN Nagar. It would also be great if all the final year MBBS students and 150 house surgeons of the medical college were immediately sent to MN Nagar for random sampling and testing of the cardiac and respiratory systems among the residents of MN Nagar. We could also inform the Indian Medical Association and put as many doctors as possible on the field to carry out the tests as quickly as possible. This may be treated as "utmost urgent" and top priority,' said Vikram after his long list of instructions.

'Yes, sir. Will start the work right away,' said an enthusiastic dean.

Vikram then called the district environment engineer, belonging to the pollution control board. 'Do you have a history of complaints regarding the functioning of the Everest Chemical Factory?'

'No, sir. They are generally compliant with all the rules and regulations.'

'Have you documented their emissions for this month?'

'Yes, sir. We did that five days ago, and it was well within the permissible limits.'

'Then do one thing, form a team right away and do a surprise check on the factory and the adjoining areas. Also, mail me all the documentation so far,' ordered Vikram.

Vikram put his appropriate machinery to work and switched on the television. Laxmipur was again making headlines. By the time Vikram had switched on the TV, the media had announced the cause of the heart attacks. The gas leak from the Everest Factory was responsible for the whole disaster; they ran animated videos of the sequence of events that led to the disaster, and how the money to the factory ownership was allegedly transferred from overseas shell accounts. Some channels alleged a link between the Opposition party and the factory, while others linked the factory ownership to the ruling party. They were also posting pictures and videos about how rich Manish

Kumar, the owner of the factory, was, and how he liked to splurge money. They repeatedly showed his daughter's lavish wedding as the anchor shouted, 'Where did this money come from?' at the top of his voice.

Vikram was actually amused seeing all that. He was recalling his famous Q & A with RPR and recollected the kind of stories that were aired back then.

Raghu came to his telephone. 'How's the situation?' enquired Vikram.

'Getting worse, sir; more people are joining in the protest. It is getting unruly,' replied Raghu.

'Is the public also joining it?'

'No, sir, most of them are from the Youth for Politics (YFP) political outfit, a few are from fringe Opposition parties, no one among the common people per se, sir.'

'Have you briefed it to your superiors about it?'

'Yes, sir, they asked me to discuss the matter with you and take a call, sir.'

'Come on, discuss then! What do you really want to do?'

'These people are unnecessarily creating a scene for their political gains, sir.'

'I asked you what you want to do about it. What do they actually deserve?'

'A sound thrashing, sir!'

'I will be there in twenty minutes; call for ten times the force you have, and keep them ready.'

'We are yet to establish a direct relation between the factory and the serial heart attacks. We don't have any concrete evidence other than the fact that the factory is close to MN Nagar, which has the maximum number of affected people. So, let's disperse and go home now. I myself will go to seal this factory if concrete evidence is found,' announced Vikram loudly into the microphone speaker.

'Corporate Dog,' came a voice from the crowd. 'How much did Manish Kumar pay you?' came another.

'Same as what you have been paid to bark by your party leadership,' replied Vikram over his mic.

Vikram looked at Raghu.

Raghu gave a thumbs-up, suggesting everything was in place to forcefully control the mob.

Vikram called out again on the mic, 'Who the hell is your leader? I want to talk to him.'

The crowd slowly gave way to a figure approaching the stage. Vikram identified the face at once and was utterly shocked.

'Jaidev!' he cried.

'Why are you even here? What are you doing with these people? Leave that group and come to my jeep,' Vikram was stunned seeing his good, old friend Jaidev and couldn't control his emotions.

'Sorry, Vikram. This is not the academy, and we are not friends anymore! I quit the system a long time ago.'

Vikram wanted to convince him to rethink his stance.

But he realized that Jaidev wouldn't give in this time.

'Even if we are not friends any more, at least let's not become enemies. Listen to me, Jaidev!'

'Of course, we are enemies when we stand on opposite sides of a fight,' shouted Jaidev at the top of his voice. His voice was filled with hatred.

'Okay, Jaidev! Good luck! All of you, listen! This is your last warning. I will count to ten. Whoever doesn't disperse from here at the count of ten will be arrested straightaway. Don't blame me later,' Vikram announced clearly.

He started counting. As he reached five, a huge stone was hurled at him and hit the glass pane of Vikram's jeep. A second one hit Bahadur who was standing right behind Vikram. Two stones were enough for Vikram to look at Raghu, and that was the cue for Raghu to unleash his forces on the mob.

What ensued over the next 15 minutes was a complete drubbing of the mob by the police. Most of them ran away while some of them got arrested. Jaidev, too, was arrested and remanded by the police.

Vikram tried to go to the police station and talk to Jaidev, but he turned his back on Vikram.

'I'm fighting for a larger cause now! And I'm a real fighter, not just a "paper fighter" like you bureaucrats,' was the only thing that he said before walking away from Vikram.

Vikram realized around 5 p.m. that he hadn't gone for the morning run that day. He also realized that he had not responded to any of Veda's calls or texts that day. He hurriedly called her, remembering his 'serious' lapses.

'What is with you? Why do you take your work so seriously, ya?' Veda remarked.

'No, it's not like that, Veda. The situation was really beyond my control, so I couldn't call!' Vikram tried to explain.

'Can you not send a simple good morning message? For every two paragraphs I type, you reply with one "okay" or a "hmmm". Now even that has stopped, which means…?' she questioned.

'Can we meet at the park now, over amla juice?' Vikram asked abruptly.

There was a pause at the other end, followed by an indistinct murmur. Veda followed it up with, 'Okay! Fine!'

Half an hour later, Vikram and Veda were sitting on the stone bench under their favourite tree in the park and were sipping their favourite amla juice.

'See, if I don't respond to your message, it doesn't mean I disrespect you or anything,' Vikram said. 'In fact, it's not at all about disrespecting, it's about caring and…'

'…and what else?' asked Vikram.

'How do I know? You need to tell! What this is, or *if* this at all is...'

'Okay! You really want me to say it. Yes, I'm in love with you! From the very first day when we started jogging together,' said Vikram in a firm tone.

'You could have said that in a more romantic way. I think this is why you haven't had a girlfriend yet! You think that you have to be the IAS officer 24 x 7, no!' Veda couldn't contain her happiness, as she teased Vikram.

'It's okay if I have never had a girlfriend. I have you now, no?'

'That's much better, boss! I too love...'

They were interrupted by the sudden influx of vehicles and their sirens around the park.

RPR strode into the park, clapping loudly.

'*Waaah rey waaah*! Vikram and Veda under a tree! And it's a love story! *Shabaaash*!' he mocked. 'The whole town is burning! There is a huge disaster striking us, but you just don't seem to care. You are busy romancing in this park, that too, with my family doctor!'

'What's your problem now, sir? Me romancing or me romancing your family doctor?' Vikram asked, still in a good mood after proposing to Veda.

'This idiot knows exactly how to spoil my moments!' Veda murmured, standing next to him.

'See! The entire town knows that the Everest Factory is responsible for the series of heart attacks! Don't try to protect anyone. Just go and seal that factory and get that Manish Kumar arrested immediately. I have already ensured the release of the innocent people whom you overstepped and arrested today,' RPR said. 'Sir, there is still no evidence against Everest...'

RPR cut him short. 'See, elections are due in just three months! I cannot take any risk now! Just shut up and do what I say! I want you to seal that factory immediately and arrest its owner. Only then will this heart-attack problem subside. Otherwise, they will raise fingers at the government's incompetence to contain this situation!'

'But sir...'

'Do you bloody want to see the sunrise tomorrow or not? You better ensure both the things are done!' RPR was at his threatening best as he turned around even without waiting for Vikram's response, twirled his moustache, and walked away.

'Now I have lost my job as his family doctor too,' Veda cribbed.

'My life is under threat, you idiot!' Vikram said.

'You will take care of all that!' Veda blushed and continued, 'this idiot ruined our romantic moment, and that I cannot tolerate.'

Just then, Vikram's phone rang. It was Raghu.

'Ya, Raghu!'

'Sir, regarding the arrest of Manish and sealing the Everest premises...'

'I only have half the reports that I had wanted, Raghu; the doctors will complete their survey tomorrow, and the pollution control board will give its final report tomorrow.'

'The pollution board has given their report already, sir. It says that over the last week, the emissions in the factory were beyond permissible limits and dangerous too.'

'But in the afternoon, the engineer had cleared the reports and said that he would submit the official report tomorrow.'

'Everything has changed now, sir. The collector has also ordered for the closure of the factory and the arrest of Manish Kumar, sir.'

Vikram hung up without saying anything.

'It is not right! Everything is going in the wrong direction. Something somewhere is extremely wrong,' he mused.

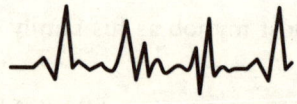

8

Tighter Knots

It was well past 8 a.m., and Vikram was still in bed. He was thinking about the things happening around him. He didn't know whom to believe and whom not to. He felt bogged down and suffocated. He felt that he had all the power, yet had none. All odds were against him, and the worst thing was that he didn't even know what to do.

'Good morning, girlfriend,' he made his first call of the day to Veda.

'Good morning, boyfriend,' Veda said with a smile. 'Last evening was awesome! Would have been even better if not for that creature that came to the park to bark.'

'Ha! Ha! We will have our time too.'

'You are not even going for your runs these days? Why are you taking these things so seriously?'

'How can I not take it seriously? It's a grave situation, and I don't even know what to do.'

'Don't do anything! Take one situation at a time; don't be so proactive; just react well to that particular situation. You can still succeed. That's what we do all the time.'

'Hmmm.'

'I will lose ₹5,000 a month now. RPR's people had called. They have fixed up a new doctor. More than the money, I will miss visiting his mother. She is a very nice person. They also had a sweet dog with whom Timmy used to play every day. Now, all of that is gone,' she cribbed. 'Okay, okay! Got to go now. Bye! Muaaah!' she hung up.

'Bye.'

Despite all the doubts and confusions on Vikram's mind, he was sure about two things—one, that Everest Factory was wrongly accused; and two, RPR was the worst person he had ever come across. He doubted if he would meet a more cunning, arrogant and abusive person in his life again.

Soon, he got up slowly from his bed, musing on the incidents surrounding him. Those were the only things on Vikram's mind, as he got ready for work.

He called the dean as soon as he reached his office.

'Sir, the good news is that there have been no new cases of the mysterious cardiac ailments since yesterday morning. We can safely assume that the serial heart attacks have stopped!'

'For now.'

'Hopefully, it won't reoccur ever, sir. It was too painful to witness everything.'

'I, too, wish that it never comes back, but you never

know. Keep assessing the cause. Do not stop that work at any cost.'

'Yes, sir.'

'What about the evaluation and survey at MN Nagar? Is that over?'

'We deployed more than 500 personnel—doctors, nurses, para medical staff, etc.—on the field, sir. There are about 35,000 households in MN Nagar, and every person covered about 50 houses yesterday. We have completed the evaluation and survey.'

'What are the findings? What did the doctors infer?'

'There were about 50–60 cases of the mysterious heart ailment from this particular area—the highest in the city. Yet, almost everyone else, who were evaluated, were found to be normal.'

'So, does that mean the emissions from Everest had no impact?'

'Yeah! That's the most likely inference that we can draw from the reports.'

After hanging up, Vikram called PA Ahmed and enquired about the findings of his team.

'We did a door-to-door survey, sir. There were no complaints of abnormal odour or difficulty in breathing. Their complaints were the usual—about the roads and the garbage.'

'Okay.'

Vikram got a WhatsApp call from Mahadev.

'Good morning, sir.'

'Good…morning…Vikram,' said Mahadev with a pause after every word as he munched on something. 'You must be feeling really bad, aren't you?' he continued.

'Not really, sir. I know it's a part and parcel of the job. We can't have everything going our way.'

'Correct! Hence, I took that quick decision and passed those orders; I'm sure you wouldn't have ordered shutting the factory down yourself. And by now, RPR would have hurt you and still got his job done by asking me to execute the orders. I saved you!'

'And what if I had already passed my orders against what he wanted, sir?'

'Well, in that case, he would have asked me to override your orders and pass fresh ones.'

'I really don't know what to say, sir. You have tried to help me, but I doubt it will be of any good, sir.'

'Don't say anything! Just be calm. The elections are coming up. Talk to the Election Commission, take a transfer, and go to a peaceful place. The Election Commission will surely consider your request, as you have genuine reasons to seek a transfer.'

Vikram did not say anything.

'Okay, son. Take care.' Mahadev hung up and resumed his munching.

Vikram then switched on the TV. RPR was on air, giving an interview.

'It is purely because of the steps taken by our government that the mysterious heart disease has been controlled. I have single-handedly stopped the serial heart attacks through my strong leadership,' he boasted.

'Sir, do you think that the serial heart attacks were due to emissions from the Everest Factory?'

'Of course yes! That's what all the official reports say. The Opposition party permitted the factory to function during its regime. God knows how much money the Opposition party leader and the then minister Manoj Kumar ji would have made in granting permission to this factory,' he claimed.

'How's your equation with the new SDM, sir? We all know about that infamous interview in Mussoorie, and now we are hearing reports that you threatened him at a park last night?'

'Did he complain or say anything about this?'

'No, sir.'

'Then, simply stop assuming things. He is obeying my orders and is completely in my control. The action taken against Everest is a testimony of it.'

Vikram tried to change the channel, but everyone was playing the RPR interview. He was doing a thorough round of chest-thumping lies!

Vikram didn't feel like working that day. He left the office, took his jeep and drove straight to Blue Line hospital.

'Is Dr Veda there?'

'Do you have an appointment?'

'No.'

'Then ma'am will not be able to see you, sir!' the hospital attendant stated, but then recognized Vikram.

'Oh! You are SDM Saab, *hai na?*'

'Ya.'

'Come, sir. I will take you to her room. Ma'am is always talking about you and your achievements, sir,' said the attendant, as he opened the door of Veda's room.

'Hey!' Veda cried cheerfully.

She dropped the stethoscope on an unassuming patient as she got up and walked towards Vikram. She held his hands and brought him to a couch at the corner of her room.

'You know what? I was really worried about you. I generally don't worry about things, but after listening to what you said this morning, I got anxious,' she said.

'Excuse me!' called out the patient, a man into his forties on whom Veda had just dropped her stethoscope and one whose existence she had completely forgotten about for a few minutes.

'Oh, I'm really sorry, sir. Give me a couple of minutes, Vikram,' she said and attended to the patient.

Vikram saw a bottle of juice on the table. He took the bottle and sipped away happily.

'Hey! Why are you drinking that?'

'If you can drink water from my glass in my office, I too can drink juice from your bottle!' taunted Vikram lovingly.

'Fool! That's Timmy's drink,' she burst out laughing.

'Er...well... But it tastes good,' said Vikram sheepishly.

'It does! I give the best health drink to Timmy! I don't have time in the morning to prepare the mix, so I make it here and send its to Timmy.'

'Oh!'

'Only oh? You can say a few nice things about my Timmy too.'

'Ha ha! Timmy is a nice dog!' said Vikram unable to think of anything to say.

'Hey! You don't like Timmy, do you? Tell me the truth! You should like him.'

'Okay, okay! I will like your Timmy! But I have a doubt.'

'What is it?'

'Does Timmy drink from the bottle directly? Like I did?'

'No, no!' Veda was still not convinced that Vikram would like Timmy.

'Anyway! You learn to like Timmy. That's all I will say. Okay, what will you have? Drink or eat?'

'I think I have had enough.'

'No, no, you should have something. We will order something.'

'Some other juice. Other than what Timmy drinks.'

'We won't get amla juice here. How about watermelon?'

'Yeah. Watermelon sounds good!'

'By the way, I'm not having amla juice these days; it reminds me too much of you. About time you resumed jogging in the mornings. Stop your excuses!'

'I will! I actually came here to tell you something.'

'What?'

'I love you, Veda. I love you so much. I wanted to completely live in the moment that we created yesterday. I want to redo it now.'

Before he could complete the sentence, Veda got up from her seat, walked up to him and kissed him.

'I, too, love you, Vikram. I love you too much! My heart is brimming with my love for you,' Veda said with tears in her eyes.

'I am glad we are able to relive the magic of that moment again. I wish we are able to relive them forever!'

Just then, the door opened. The nurse came in and said, 'Ma'am, the chief has started the rounds five minutes ago and has already asked for you twice.'

'Oh my god! These people will never leave us in peace,' cribbed Veda.

'Can you please wait for half an hour? I really want to have lunch with you,' she begged Vikram.

'Don't worry! Take your time. I'll wait. We will have lunch together once you are back,' he said.

'Sure, sure! I will try to sneak out. If not, we will order in, okay?'

'Okay, okay,' said Vikram.

After Veda reluctantly walked out of the room, Vikram switched on the TV.

'Thankfully, there won't be any breaking news on the

TV about Laxmipur for now!' he said, as he switched on the TV in a slightly relaxed mood.

'Drama in Laxmipur,' read the ticker in bold letters!

'Holy f#@*!'

'What's this now?' he said, as the headlines flashed on the screen.

'IT raids at over three hundred places in Laxmipur. This has to be the most massive raid in the history of UP. The Opposition MLA and ex-minister Manoj Kumar's house among the top people whose houses are being raided currently,' said the anchor.

'Thankfully, I don't have anything to do with this, nor do I have to do anything about it! Good!' He remarked and switched channels to check if RPR was being raided, but sadly couldn't find it.

The Opposition MLA Manoj Kumar was addressing the press as the raids were going on in his house.

'This is pure political vendetta. The ruling state party and their major ally, the central ruling party, have colluded and have staged this to weaken us before the elections. We will not budge to all this drama. We are true to ourselves. We are pure, and we will come out clean,' he protested.

There were continuous visuals of the major commercial establishments; important people's houses were being raided.

Laxmipur was in the limelight yet again, for all the wrong reasons. There was breaking news about Laxmipur every other day. The topsy-turvy turn of things in close proximity to the elections made way for lots and lots of speculations, discussions and rumours among people of all walks except one man—the one who knew that he had full control over things. He was drinking away, watching the news about the IT raids in his bungalow with all his party cadres and laughing loudly.

'All this is nothing! The worst is yet to come!' he roared, twirling his moustache.

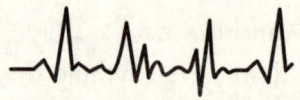

9

Gathering Storm

'By the time this land acquisition process is through, I hope I don't retire from the service!' Vikram was signing away files in his chamber, with Ahmed standing next to him.

He glanced at the monthly report from the dean, which said that the mysterious cardiac illness that had lasted about 24 hours had completely stopped and no new cases had been reported after those bizarre 24 hours.

Bahadur opened the door and seemed rather tense. 'Sir, the people from the United Front for Temples (UFFT) have come,' he said.

'What's with these people? Every second day I get some *tappal* from them?'

'They are troublemakers, sir. All they do is create problems in the name of religion. Our office has had a lot of bad experiences with them in the past, sir,' said Ahmed.

'Which political party do they side with?' asked Vikram.

'Whichever party favours them!' came the reply.

'Okay, let them in,' he told Bahadur.

Soon, a group of 50–60 people entered Vikram's chamber. The sudden influx of so many people made Vikram's otherwise-large office chamber look rather small.

All of them looked uncouth, spoke roughly and behaved boorishly—pushing chairs out of their way, objects on the table and occupying the entire room. The room was so full of people that the door couldn't be closed, and there were people waiting outside too.

'Namaste, sir,' said their headman in the most disrespectful manner.

'Ya, tell me,' said Vikram.

'This is regarding our procession.'

'Yeah, I have seen your representations. You have been creating only trouble in the guise of processions every year.'

'Sir, so are you opposing god?' started Rakhi, their headman.

'When did I say that? I said you are disturbing the peace of this land in the name of all your processions.'

'Don't accuse us, sir.'

'I am not accusing anyone. I have a job to do and I am being paid for that. You can have your procession but stick to the route that we assign to you. Do not take your own routes,' said Vikram sternly.

'Our route is what we want, sir.'

'Why?'

'You will not understand our emotions. It is all about showing who *we* are in front of *them*,' he said in a vengeful voice.

'Who *are* you all? I simply don't understand. Merely caste, religion or class doesn't define you. It's what you work for and become in life that defines you,' said Vikram.

'Your reformatory speeches will not work with us. Those before you had tried such tactics as well,' said another bald man who was standing next to Rakhi.

'Your intimidations don't work with me either! This is my office, and you will do things my way. If you want my permission, you need to stick to my route. My PA will give you the route map, sign on it and leave! Understood? You can all go now!' Vikram ordered.

'Are you threatening us?'

'Yes! Now what? Get out before I do something really nasty!'

'First, he advised, then ordered; if these people are adamant, he will surely use force,' Bahadur laughed to himself.

Rakhi and their 'select' leaders looked and each other and left the room extremely annoyed. Some of them pounded the door and walls as they left the room, slamming the door behind them.

Ahmed came in a few minutes later. 'They have signed on the route, sir,' he said with a sigh of relief.

'How do you pick your clothes for office?' asked Veda curiously.

Vikram and Veda were back to their morning jogs. They were cruising along their usual route, chatting and laughing along.

'Why do you ask?'

'Because you repeat most of your clothes,' she said.

'I pick up whatever lies on top of the pile. It is simple and saves a lot of time!' he laughed.

'I guessed so!'

'How do you choose your clothes?' asked Vikram.

'Well, that's a good question. I actually wanted you to ask me this question!'

'Ha ha! Go ahead!'

'I usually pick the colour of my nails for the week.'

'What has that got to do with the dress?'

'Everything, SDM Saab! I match the colours with that of my clothes for the week! For jogging, office and everything. See?' she proudly showed off her yellow-coloured nails, which went with the bright yellow t-shirt she was wearing for her morning jogs.

'So you actually sit and plan these things?' Vikram was seriously surprised.

'*Aur kya?*' Veda was not so pleased with Vikram's response.

'See, you should like my love for clothes and for Timmy! Whether you like it or not!' she started laughing.

'Should I like them or not?'

'Like! Like!'

'I like everything about you, not just your love for clothes and your dog. Everything about you is very lovable!'

Veda didn't say anything. She was too overwhelmed to utter even a word. Suddenly, both of them stopped and looked deep into each other's eyes. There was that spark in them, brimming with love and happiness. Anyone who saw them would say that they were truly in love with each other.

They both burst into laughter after staring into each other's eyes for a few minutes, standing in the middle of the road, in front of the bus stand and started running again.

'I don't see you talk to your friends much. Why is that?' asked Veda.

'I have always been very selective about friends. My career too didn't give much room for friends—both in media and as a bureaucrat. Rakesh and Jaidev had always been very good friends. Jaidev was deeply traumatized after the events at LBSNAA. He had been off radar, but I had never expected to see him the way I did the other day. Rakesh, too, was badly hurt that time. But he has always be a cool dude! He has clearly risen over it and is doing really well now.'

'It's the same with me. There are only a handful of friends from college with whom I'm close to. Otherwise, I stick to casual chit-chats with most people.'

'Hmmm. So no more mysterious cardiac cases nowadays?' enquired Vikram.

'No! It all happened within twenty-four hours! Nothing after that,' she said.

'What do you think could have been the reason?'

'I don't know. Not sure. Frankly, I haven't seen anything like this in my life. And, I don't subscribe to this factory gas inhalation theory,' she said.

'I too don't subscribe to it, but then, we don't have a counter theory.'

'Anyway, I'm glad that it's over. Memories of that day still continue to haunt me.'

'Having seen it all, I am proud of what you did that day…how you saved lives!'

'Boss, we do that every day!'

'Accepted! And I also think it's time for you to get to the life-saver mode! Time for me to get ready for office too!' said Vikram, looking at his watch.

'Call me after you reach office! Bye! Muah.'

'What is with these UFFT people, Raghu? Why are they hell-bent on creating trouble?'

'They have always been like that, sir. All of their work and activities have ulterior motives.'

'Do they listen to RPR?'

'Sometimes they do, sir, sometimes they don't. We never know, sir. They are thorough opportunists,' said Raghu.

'Will they convene the procession peacefully today and as per our agreement? They have signed on it, remember!'

Raghu started laughing. 'Sir, you are an intelligent person. Do you really think they care about that agreement? They will do it their way only, sir, and they will create trouble! That's how they are! Let alone us, even our institution cannot lay a finger on them! But good thing you tried to make them fall in line. Had you refused to meet them, they would have gone to the DM and got the permission,' said Raghu.

'Let's see. I have spoken to our DM, SP, and those of the neighbouring district for additional support. We will deploy five times the police force on the route of their procession. Rakhi and Co. can try whatever they want,' Vikram was gearing up for a tough day.

'Their procession will commence in the evening. Assemble the team and be ready on the spot. Do keep me updated. Good luck!' Vikram sent out clear orders.

It was time for the procession to begin. Raghu took his position. There were about 150 people participating in the procession. All men, no women or children. The idol was placed on a palanquin with minimal decor. All of them in the procession were chanting loudly, and these chants were coupled with drumbeats that echoed like thunder.

'You sure there are no women or children?' asked Vikram.

'No, sir, there aren't,' Raghu was reporting from the ground, amidst the noise.

'Is Rakhi, the bald guy, or any of the leaders there?'

'No, sir! I, too, was looking for them, but they aren't to be seen in this procession, sir.'

'These are signs of danger. They are having a supposed social gathering without women, children or their leaders, which means only one thing—trouble! Stay alert and keep me updated. I'm in touch with the SP too.'

'Yes, sir.'

Vikram couldn't contain his anxiety. He had been quite anxious over the past one month. Now he was facing another situation. He wondered where this would take him when he got a call from Raghu.

'Sir, they are taking a different route, sir! They have taken a sharp turn right after the mosque, and have entered the neighbourhood, sir. They are not listening to us; they are pushing our people. I spoke to the SP; he told me to ask for your opinion about further action,' reported Raghu.

'Is it very bad? Will they listen if we talk?'

'No sir, they are pushing our men. Also, they are attacking bystanders randomly. They are beating up a civilian as we speak. Shall we go ahead, sir?'

'Yes! Plan B it is! You know what to do! Pulp them!'

'All right, sir!'

―⌇―

Vikram got a call again in precisely seven minutes. It was from Raghu. Vikram took the call even before his phone finished ringing the first time.

'They are using knives and daggers, sir! A couple of our men have been injured! Do we have your order to shoot, sir? Can we proceed? We are waiting, sir!'

'No no, wait. Shots in the air only! Proceed no further than that. Don't use any of the modern guns. They hardly make a sound. Use our good old 303 rifles and shoot a few times in the air! This will disperse the people.'

'Okay, sir.'

Vikram was feeling numb after he hung up. So many permutations and combinations were running through his mind. He knew that this situation wouldn't be a pleasant one, but had never expected a disaster of this kind. He was seriously hoping that they did not open fire on people.

He held on to his phone and waited for the call impatiently. Vikram's heart was beating fast. He switched on the TV to see if the news had already broken.

'Thankfully, there is nothing on the TV yet,' he said.

Raghu called again.

'Sir, we shot in the air continuously as instructed and most of them scattered away.'

'Are any civilians injured?'

'No, sir.'

'Good.'

'But, sir...'

'What?'

'As they were dispersing and the crowd was thinning

out, Rakhi and the bald man came out with daggers, sir...'

'Oh my!'

'...and they started attacking the bystanders like maniacs, sir.'

'Then?'

'We did not use fire as clearly instructed by you and SP sir.'

'What happened next?'

'Our men had to engage in a combat with them with our lathis, sir.'

'Oh! Are our people hurt?'

'Yes, sir, but they are all right. But...'

'What?'

'Rakhi and the bald man are dead, sir.'

'What?'

'Did our men engage with them only with lathis?' Vikram continued in disbelief.

'Yes, sir.'

'This is F*#ing unbelievable!' cried an astonished Vikram.

Just then, the news broke on the TV.

10
The Burst

'The dates for the Assembly Elections will be announced any moment in UP. The entire state is gripped by the election fever. Preparations for the elections by the prominent parties are in full swing…'

Ashok Kumar Pandey was listening to the news bulletin on the radio.

Ashok Kumar Pandey, popularly known as A.K. Pandey, was one of the oldest and senior-most politicians of the state. He was one of the first impactful politicians to hail from Laxmipur. He used to be a very outspoken and bold politician. He tried to be as honest as possible, despite facing the odds most of the time. His role in the growth of the ruling party was truly critical and commendable. Now, he was nearing his eighties; he was frail, 'retired' from politics and had been mostly confined to his house for almost a decade.

The period of A.K. Pandey's 'home confinement' coincided with the meteoric rise of RPR as one of the most powerful politicians of the state. In fact, A.K. Pandey was the one who had recommended the first MLA ticket for RPR. He had been RPR's mentor at that time. The rise of RPR meant a lot of avenues of conflict with A.K. Pandey. After a point, RPR had grown beyond the control of A.K. Pandey. He had become the only person who stood between RPR and his wild and greedy dreams. That was when RPR used his money and muscle to sideline Pandey.

Pandey was brought down, one-step at a time, to a point where he no longer cared about the party or his future in politics. It was at that juncture that he decided to 'leave' everything and spend whatever time he had left in peace. He wrote occasionally when he was reminiscent of his old self, but as time went by, he even gave up writing. He was living a reclusive life all by himself, watching the world go by him. Though physically still fit, Pandey was mentally not sound and had become a pale shadow of his former self.

Pandey had been feeling quite uneasy since morning. He was having his usual meal of curd rice, pickle and papad and listening to the news on the radio. Just when he was about to pick a handful of rice, he saw a few drops of blood on the curd rice. He had been feeling his chest tightening up for the past half an hour. Initially, he had been trying to bear and overcome the pain, but now it had become unbearable. Pandey put his hands on his nose to find both his nostrils bleeding profusely. In a matter of seconds, the curd rice had turned red and Pandey fell right onto it.

He was no more.

'Everyone is calling you the daredevil of your division!' Shankar started at his 'modest' best, praising Shamitha and belittling her in his mind as to how she was only a show off and had not really achieved anything so far. On the other hand, he was quite pleased with the way things were going for him, and he was becoming a hero.

'Hmmm. No, yaar! You are being celebrated as the darling of the masses. Everyone is very appreciative of your initiatives. You have a good media coverage as well, since you are posted at the headquarter subdivision,' Shamitha's fake praises pleased Shankar.

Shankar, Shamitha, Rakesh and Vikram were on a conference call catching up with each other.

'Rakesh, we heard that you are on a long leave? Why yaar?'

'His stand-up shows have been huge hits. He even performed in Laxmipur, which was attended by about a thousand people,' said Vikram.

'Is that so? That's greaaaaattt!' cried Shamitha, thinking what a loser Rakesh was, to perform after becoming an IAS officer.

Shankar, on the other hand, was slightly happy as Rakesh was concentrating on other things. This meant one person less to compete with. Nevertheless, Shankar gave his customary congratulatory message to Rakesh in an emotional yet fakest possible way.

'Thanks, guys!' said Rakesh. 'I'm living my life my way! I'm starting my own production company soon,' he said.

A round of fake appreciation followed.

'I will share it in the state IAS group and our batch's group,' said a selfless Shankar.

'Hey Vikram! What's up with you? Still not hearing good things about you, man.' The enthusiasm in Shankar's voice, as he uttered those words, was evident!

Vikram was sitting on the couch in Veda's room at the hospital. It was a holiday and incoming patients were lesser compared to other days. Veda was sitting next to him and was listening to the conversation on the speaker.

'That's okay, man! As long you keep hearing about me!' replied Vikram.

'Did the minister threaten you in the park too?' he asked curiously.

'Who told you?'

'I think I read about it in some magazine.'

Vikram started laughing.

'We should keep these politicians under control, yet be cordial with them. That's what I have been doing,' said Shamitha.

'Even I am very strict. My Mantri is actually slightly scared of me, as I directly communicate with the CM.' It was Shankar's moment to go up a notch on Shamitha.

Rakesh and Vikram just kept quiet.

'It was sad and disappointing to see Jaidev! He put in so much of hard work to get to this level, and then to end up like this is terrible,' said Shamitha.

'Has he been bailed out?' asked Rakesh.

'Ya, he had been released the same day,' replied Vikram.

'I should talk to him,' said Shamitha with no intention whatsoever of talking to him again in life.

'The elections are due. I think these people will surely come back,' said Shankar.

'Ya ya, surely! They will come back. I have been hearing that RPR could be one of the chief ministerial candidates this time,' added Shamitha.

'Be careful, Vikram. Don't keep rubbing him the wrong way. It's only for your good that we are telling this,' said Shankar.

'Yes, Vikram. Please be careful…even during the elections,' Shamitha said in a sympathetic tone.

Vikram just said 'Hmm…' after a delayed pause.

'What do these people want? I mean, why are they like this?' Veda asked Vikram in a surprised tone after he had hung up.

'Ha ha! They have always been this way. Rakesh is fine.

'The other two are extremely funny,' Vikram said.

'I think they are more slanderous than funny,' remarked Veda.

'Well, that depends on how we take it. There are many like these two in my fraternity. This is why I don't take these guys seriously. Just enjoy their chest-beating, fake modesty and austerity. These things really lights up my day! It's actually funny, you know!' said Vikram.

'Funny or not, with people like RPR and these guys, I am glad that you are taking it all in your stride. I have seen you depressed at times, but you have tried to put that away and move on. I truly admire you for that, Vikram,' Veda spoke with empathy.

Vikram got a call even before he could react to Veda's appreciations. It was from the dean.

'What? Is it?' was the familiar shock response from Vikram.

'Send a red alert to all hospitals and issue instructions to strictly follow treatment protocols. No more loss of life this time,' he instructed the dean.

'What happened? Please don't tell me that the heart attack outbreak is back,' Veda asked in a worried tone.

'Yes and no,' replied Vikram.

'Meaning?'

'Meaning that there has been a new case of the mysterious heart disease. Pandey, the senior politician, was affected and has lost his life. Outbreak or not, we will find out soon.'

Veda rushed to check for new cases admitted to the emergency room.

A.K. Pandey's body was placed in a freezer box at the centre of his house, where various dignitaries came to offer their condolences. RPR had placed the flower wreath on his body, slowly turning around to face the cameras, as he wiped his tears. Just then, RPR's sidekick came in waddling through the crowd with a phone in his hand.

'Sir! CM Saab is on the line,' he said.

'Namaste, Saab!' RPR grabbed the phone from his hand and walked away from the hall as he spoke to the CM.

'We are preparing a list of officials who are to be transferred before the elections. Who all are to be replaced in your district?' the CM asked.

'Don't change the SDM, Saab. I will send you the list for the others,' replied RPR.

'Are you sure? I know you will win easily but do you really want that guy there? He already tried to damage your reputation!'

'That's exactly why I want him here. List of other officials to be transferred will be sent to you right away, *ji*.'

RPR told his sidekick to call Vikram right away.

'SDM Saab! How are you?' he asked.

'I'm good, sir.'

'Elections are round the corner in. We need to prepare a list of officials who are to be transferred. CM Saab asked me regarding your transfer too.'

There was no reply from Vikram's end.

'You know what?' RPR started teasing him again.

Vikram was already annoyed with the recurrence of the mysterious heart ailment. He was frustrated for not being able to make headway and ensure its control, and now, he was being teased and cornered.

Vikram had been simmering with anger all along as RPR continued to bully him.

'You know what?' RPR continued, 'I want you to be here for the elections. You will anyway be the returning officer, and I will win emphatically. I want you to see all that. Feel helpless, feel impotent and then hand over the victory certificate to me. Once you have endorsed my victory and witnessed the people's support, you will be transferred out of my district. You will hand over my victory certificate and I will hand over your transfer order. I will crush you and throw you away,' a venom-spewing RPR spoke.

'You know what, sir. For every crime you have been committing, I will ensure that you are brought before the law and are suitably punished! That will be the moment you will experience the very feelings that you have always wanted me to feel! These words are of an honest public servant who wants to do good for the people. They will come true!' Vikram burst out like a lion.

RPR disconnected the call and threw it at his sidekick.

'He will know what pain is after the elections,' RPR roared.

Vikram was breathing heavily after he hung up. It felt like he was breathing fire.

Veda opened the door and came in just then.

'Thankfully, there aren't any more cases at our hospital. Also, I just checked with other major hospitals. They too haven't got new cases,' she said with a sigh of relief.

Just then, Vikram got another call. He was fuming as he picked up the phone.

'Hello,' he said in a harsh tone.

'Sir? This is the dean.'

'Ya, tell me,' Vikram was trying to contain himself.

'The autopsy reports of Rakhi and his accomplice Nandan have arrived,' said the dean.

'Okay!'

'They do not have major internal bruises or injuries, sir. Instead, they have congestions in their heart vessels and pulmonary edema, which clearly seemed to have been the cause of their deaths, sir.'

'Holy f#@*! This means…'

'This means Rakhi and his accomplice did not succumb to injuries suffered in the riots, sir. They died of heart attacks—the same mysterious heart disease that has been claiming lives in Laxmipur.'

Vikram knew that the time had come for him to take

things into his hands. Until now, he had been reacting to situations and providing the best support, but now was the time to become proactive. Now was the time to stand up and deliver. Now was the time for action...

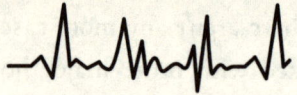

11

Trail Times

'Did you cross-check the autopsy findings of Rakhi and Nandan with that of the earlier victims of the heart disease?' asked Vikram.

'Yes, sir. The cause of death is the same,' replied the dean.

Vikram was sitting in his office on a Sunday evening and breaking his head over the issue.

'Do all the findings match with that of Pandey's as well?' asked Vikram.

'Yes, sir.'

'Let's try comparing Pandey, Rakhi and Nandan only for now. I had told you to track their medical history, food habits, etc. Could you find anything from them?'

'Not yet, sir.'

'Stop being a typical government servant—doing things in a routine manner. Learn to think out of the box. I'm sure you will be able to find answers,' Vikram was losing his patience with the dean.

Just then, Raghu walked into Vikram's office.

'Good evening, sir.'

'Good evening, Raghu. I want you to focus on the things Pandey, Rakhi and Nandan did on the day of their deaths—people they met, food they ate and places they visited. I need complete details,' Vikram instructed.

'Yes, sir,' said Raghu and handed over a pen drive.

'This pen drive has the complete video of the UFFT procession, sir. It even has portions of the riot. We had it recorded for surveillance purposes.'

'I'll have a look. You too take a look at the things that I have told you and get back to me as early as possible.'

'Yes, sir,' replied Raghu.

It was past 9 p.m. and Vikram was still in his office.

He was watching the tapes of the UFFT procession that Raghu had given him.

Before the procession had started, he noticed a vehicle stop by near the crowd. It was a van covered with promotional posters. It stopped by and a man came out and started distributing what looked like chocolates.

Vikram paused the video and zoomed in on the chocolates. They read 'Honey Squeeze Chocolates'. The crowd gathered around him as he handed out the chocolates and the people started eating them. Soon, the van left and the procession started. During the course of the procession, Vikram saw Nandan eating the chocolate and giving one to Rakhi.

After some time, Vikram saw Rakhi and Nandan stopped at a tea stall. Rakhi was drinking the tea while Nandan made a phone call.

Just then, Raghu walked into Vikram's office again.

'I have spoken to Ratan, who used to be Pandey's long-time assistant, sir. That morning, Pandey's only granddaughter, Diya, was at the house with her husband and their eight-year-old daughter. They had come two days ago and had left the house around noon. Pandey had not left the house the whole week. Also, that day, he maintained his routine diet—a glass of milk in the morning, with two biscuits and curd rice in the afternoon after his daughter left. It was during his lunch that he had collapsed and passed away,' detailed Raghu.

'What about the night before? Any details?' Vikram asked. He felt like a detective suddenly.

'Ratan was out of town the previous day, sir. There is a nightwatchman at their place. Maybe, he could help us.'

'Let's go then!' Vikram got up with utmost eagerness to get to the bottom of things.

Suddenly, he was reminded of Veda's words.

'Almost every disease is detectable from the history of the patient. The patient's history speaks a lot about the aetiology of the disease. A good doctor would be able to elicit the cause of the disease from the person's history. Physical examination and laboratory diagnosis are all only secondary,' she had told Vikram.

Vikram wanted to collect the detailed history of the victims and discuss with Veda.

They reached Pandey's house. Pandey's daughter stayed abroad, but his granddaughter who was visiting him was there, rearranging things in the house. The security guard was a man in his sixties, yet strong, with grey hair and a moustache. He always had a frown on his face, but replied very politely to Vikram's questions.

'Did anything unusual happen the night before?'

'No, sir. Pandey Saab was sitting in the lawn and chatting with his eight-year-old great granddaughter.'

'Did you notice any unknown person outside the house that night or the day before?'

'No, sir.'

'Did he seem to be in good health the night before or did he seem ill?' Vikram asked.

'He seemed quite normal, sir,' replied the security guard.

Vikram and Raghu also made brief enquiries with Diya and were about to leave the place when the security guard called out to them.

'Saab! I remember something!'

'What is it?' asked Vikram. His heart was racing.

'A vehicle arrived in the evening as I had just begun my shift. I saw someone step out of it and he was distributing chocolates.'

'Oh! What exactly did they do?' Vikram asked. He, somehow, had been expecting this answer.

'The van just stopping by and giving away chocolates to the residents,' said the security guard.

'Did Pandey get the chocolates?' Vikram asked.

'No, saab. The little girl got the chocolate. But I saw them sitting in the garden and eating it together.'

'Did you see Pandey eating it?'

'Yes, sir! Normally, he doesn't eat chocolates, but that day the little girl forced him to have it. I clearly remember,' asserted the security guard.

Vikram then went to one of the neighbours and asked about the chocolates.

'They were here to promote their chocolates and were giving them away for free,' said the neighbour.

'Did you get them too?' asked Vikram.

'Yes, of course. The entire neighbourhood got it that day. All of us ate it. They were pretty good,' commented the neighbour.

'Do you have any of it left?'

'Wait. Let me check.'

The neighbour brought a couple of them.

'Here you go! Luckily, we had a few left in the refrigerator,' he said as he gave away the chocolates to Vikram.

'Thank you,' said Vikram and walked away.

'Can chocolates cause heart attacks?' Vikram immediately called Veda, without wasting much time.

'That sounds kind of weird. Why?'

'I'm asking if those mysterious heart-related deaths could be caused by chocolates?' he asked.

'Unlikely. But then, we need to look at the composition of the chocolates, study the ingredients in detail to come to a conclusion. There may be a few chemicals that may trigger arrhythmias, but it would be too far-fetched to bracket it with this case,' Veda replied.

'Ya, that's true! A lot of people have consumed the chocolates but very few of them have suffered the heart ailment. It is farfetched, but we don't have any other clue or favourable history to work with,' said Vikram

'All right. Bring the chocolates. I'll send them to the pharmaceutical lab. A friend of mine works there,' said Veda.

Vikram returned home and carefully studied the visuals again to ascertain the address on the van. All he could see was 'Honey Squeeze Chocolates'. Written in tiny letters beneath it at a few places was 'Laxmipur-67'.

Vikram had already sent out his men and asked Raghu to send out his as well, to question the participants of the procession and Pandey's neighbours to learn whatever they could about the company. However, they came back empty-handed.

'I have a clue,' Vikram said, pointing at the visual.

'Which area corresponds to the pincode 67?' he asked.

Raghu thought for a while and said, 'PNT Colony, sir.'

'Good, let's start asking the people there if they know about this chocolate company,' said Vikram.

'We will do that, sir. But are you sure about this chocolate trail, sir?' asked Raghu.

'Do we have a better option?' Vikram shot back.

'No, sir!'

'Then? See you at PNT Colony tomorrow morning,' Vikram said sharply.

He then called out to PA Ahmed, 'Prepare the list of all cases of the mysterious heart disease and track them to their addresses, and check for a history of Honey Squeeze Chocolates consumptions,' he instructed as Ahmed noted down the orders diligently.

'Get your people involved to track down the chocolate intake of the other people who were affected,' he told Raghu.

'Yes, sir,' replied Raghu.

'Let only reliable people be involved in this. Let the whole operation be confidential, and most importantly, ensure your men wear civilian clothes and carry out casual enquiries only,' Vikram instructed Raghu.

'Same goes for you too,' he told Ahmed.

Both Ahmed and Raghu agreed and left the room.

Later, Vikram tried searching the chocolate's name on the Internet, hoping to find some link, but all he got were links to chocolate websites that were based out of India.

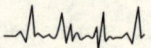

The dates for the UP state legislative assembly elections were announced, and the political parties were preparing in full swing. Vikram knew that the election process would soon begin and he would have additional responsibilities. This would affect the investigation in the case of mysterious heat attacks. He had to act, and act quickly. Vikram knew that he was up against the odds, but he was sure that he was onto something. That made him happy.

It was an extremely hot day in Laxmipur as the police officers carried on with their enquiries on the chocolate company. While some of them reported seeing the promo van, most of them denied it. However, none of them had any idea as to where or what the company was.

'How many schools and colleges are there in this area?' Vikram asked.

'No colleges, sir, but three schools,' replied Ahmed.

'Let's visit the schools. I need to talk to the kids.'

Soon, they reached one of the schools and Vikram started speaking to the kids. He told them a few motivational things and towards the end of his speech, casually asked them about the chocolates. But no one knew anything about the company.

Vikram was visiting the third and last school. He

entered the sixth grade and spoke to the students about their ambitions and aspirations. He then asked them about the makers of the Honey Squeeze Chocolates.

'I have seen its factory,' said one of the boys.

'Where have you seen it?' Vikram asked, showing him the company logo.

'I saw it when I had gone to my friend's house last Sunday to play cricket. It's right next to the graveyard in an isolated space between the graveyard and the bridge,' the boy said.

'After the game, I even went there with my friend and got a few chocolates,' he added.

'How big was the building?' asked Vikram.

'It isn't exactly a building. It was like two to three ATMs put together,' said the boy.

Soon the boy, Raghu and Vikram were walking across the graveyard towards the company.

It was getting dark and the graveyard felt eerie. The boy clung to Vikram as they walked past the graveyard in silence.

'How did you cross it that day then?' Vikram asked, trying to cheer up the boy.

'We were here in broad daylight, sir! Not at this time,' the boy replied. His breathing improved now that they had crossed the graveyard.

The boy gasped for breath when he saw what was in front of him. Vikram's heart beat faster.

There was no building in the place described by the boy.

Every other thing described by the boy was right there.

'Are you sure this was the place?' asked Vikram.

'Y...e...sss... s...iii...r,' the boy was frightened now. The shop from where he and his friend had bought chocolates last week was nowhere to be found!

Vikram got a call from Veda just then.

'Yes! Those damn chocolates contain ingredients that could f#@*ing cause arrhythmias,' Veda was almost screaming at the other end unable to control her emotions.

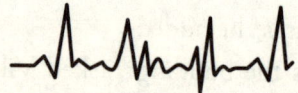

12

Shocks, Storms, Breakthroughs

'Are you sure that the chocolate contains ingredients that could trigger heart attacks?' asked Vikram.

'I would have loved to say no, but unfortunately, it's true!

'Those chocolates contain Yohimbine, heparin and clonidine, among a few other ingredients.'

'What are those?'

'Yohimbine is an alkaloid derived from the bark of trees. People with erectile dysfunction primarily use it. It's banned in many countries, as it could seriously affect the rhythm of the heart and potentially trigger a heart attack. Clonidine changes the way our body releases hormones that affect the heart, and heparin causes bleeding. There are other ingredients too, but in traces. I will need more time for a deeper research,' said Veda.

'Oh! That explains the symptoms in the people who were affected. But why were only a few of them affected out of hundreds who had eaten the chocolates?'

'The human body! Every single human body is unique! Nobody knows what happens beyond a point!' replied Veda.

Vikram, somehow, was not convinced. They had been speaking for over an hour now over the phone, and something was bugging Vikram throughout the conversation.

'Okay, Veda!' he said suddenly and sharply.

'Your "okay, Veda" means you need to hang up now, no? Tell the truth?' Veda said with a smile.

Vikram, too, smiled foolishly, as he was rightly 'caught' by Veda.

'It is this case that's eating me,' he said.

'Ya, first it was RPR, now this case!' Veda said with a hint of sarcasm.

'Anyway, I will sleep! I know you will skip jogging tomorrow! We will try to meet for lunch!' she continued.

'Ya, I will drop by your hospital for lunch. We will order in. Good night,' said Vikram

'Good night! Muah!' Veda hung up.

'Holy shit!' cried Vikram as he suddenly woke up with a brainwave. It was about eight in the morning. As Veda had guessed rightly, Vikram hadn't gone to jog and was still lying in bed, thinking about the dramatic events that had been happening over the past few days. Vikram suddenly felt that he had cracked something important in this case.

'I need the complete list of people who were raided by the income tax office and the list of people who had suffered the disease in the first spell,' Vikram told Raghu over phone from his bed.

'Yes, sir,' he replied.

'Do you have any new info?'

'There is evidence of quite a few of the people affected in the first spell by consuming Honey Squeeze Chocolates, sir.'

'Well, that isn't surprising, but good that we have confirmation and validation on that,' Vikram said.

'What about the person distributing the chocolates? Were you able to track down his details?' Vikram asked.

'We have only blurred images of his, sir. We are trying our best to match profiles with it,' replied Raghu.

'Okay, see you at the office with both the lists. That info could be crucial,' he asserted.

'All right, sir!'

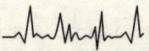

Raghu was right on time at Vikram's office.

Vikram was getting started with his election work as the nomination filing dates were nearing. RPR was to be announced as the ruling party's candidate, unopposed.

'Hi Raghu! Got the lists?' Vikram asked right away.

Raghu immediately showed the files that he was holding.

'They are here, sir,' he said.

'Good. Ahmed and a few of my trusted men are here. I would suggest you work with them. Examine the list of affected people one by one, and see if any of them are related to the people who were raided by the income tax officials. From what I have noticed, there is this guy, Kiran Kumar, who is the bus driver for the City International School. I have seen him drive the car of their chairman, who owns the City Group Hospitals. I saw that guy quite a few times when I was visiting Veda. I instantly recognized his face after seeing him at GH admitted with heart ailment. So, in his case, his chairman was also one of those who were raided and are being kept under vigil now. Likewise, I want you to check on the people who were affected by the heart disease and see if you can establish links with those in the list of people raided by the IT officials,' explained Vikram.

'If there are more such cases, this is going to be a massive breakthrough in the case, sir!' said Raghu.

'Yes! Let's see!' said Vikram.

'One more thing, sir. There is a lot of pressure from my superiors in the police department to have me do the routine work, sir. They think I'm wasting my time,' said Raghu.

'What do you think?' asked Vikram.

'This feels like one of the very few times I can do justice to this uniform, sir. That's how I feel when I'm with you, sir. Whatever the outcome may be, I'll be around you and face it, sir!' said Raghu with a touch of emotion.

Vikram smiled and got on with his election work.

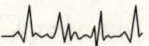

Veda had just finished ordering lunch for the two of them, using her food delivery app. 'This is nice, isn't it? Two of us ordering from two different restaurants, that too by sitting here in a hospital!' she said.

'Yeah! This is nice! Veda, I have a question,' started Vikram.

'I know you are going to ask about the mysterious heart disease and the chocolates. Come on. Shoot!' she said.

'Can someone sit elsewhere and control these heart attacks the same way we are ordering food on an app?' asked Vikram.

'What?' asked Veda, slightly astonished.

'I mean, I have heard about telemedicine and stuff. Is it possible to control a heart attack?' he clarified.

'Well, that sounds quite villainous and straight out of a science fiction novel!' she claimed.

'Is it possible?'

'Hey! My head is reeling, ya! Give me some time to think!' Veda was truly shocked hearing Vikram's theory.

'Okay, think!' said Vikram, pulling out his phone to start browsing.

Veda sat quietly, and it took her quite some time to process what Vikram had just said. The whole idea seemed villainously incredulous! She, too, picked up her laptop and went through a few files in it.

'Okay, fine! I'll tell you what I know,' she said, clearing her throat after about ten minutes.

'Go on,' Vikram said. He was waiting to hear what Veda had to say.

'See, to reduce the side-effects of chemotherapy and to increase the efficacy of the treatment, remote-controlled drugs are being tried, using nanoparticles at various levels with varying results for the treatment of cancer. These practices are more prevalent abroad. They are yet to enter the Indian market,' she said.

'So, this is possible! Remote-controlled drugs!'

'Yes. In remote-controlled chemotherapy, the nanoparticles and allied compounds, acting as both drug-delivery vehicles and as contrast agents for further investigation like the MRI,' Veda said.

'But what's the principle behind it? It sounds incredible and fictitious.'

'I just looked it up on my computer. In case of chemotherapy drugs, the drug, say cisplatin for example, is bound to the strands of the DNA, which are, in turn, bound to iron oxide spheres.'

'Okay. Chemotherapy drug plus DNA plus iron oxide spheres. The drug, as I understand, is to treat the disease, but what are DNA and iron oxide spheres for?' Vikram asked curiously.

'The DNA strand acts as a binding agent. It is used like a gum to bind the drug with iron oxides. The iron oxide spheres are the most important components. When these iron oxide spheres are heated by using radio frequency waves, the heat breaks the DNA strands, which hold the drug, and this drug is released into the blood stream,' she said.

'Oh! Now I understand! This is crazy stuff!' exclaimed Vikram.

'As the drugs are made of nanoparticles, a cocktail of drugs in large quantity could easily be given to the patient. This is for chemotherapy. If you need to induce a remote-controlled heart attack the same way, you just need to replace the chemotherapy drug nanoparticles with heart attack, inducing drugs or substances,' she said.

'Which are present in the chocolates! Holy f@#*! This is the most f@#*ing incredible thing I have ever heard!' Vikram couldn't control his astonishment.

'Holy crap! This is INSANE! So you are telling me that these mysterious heart ailments have been orchestrated?' asked Veda, with fear in her voice.

'It looks like it!' said Vikram

'These are medical murders then! Why would someone want to kill about 300 random civilians, including Pandey, Rakhi and Nandan?' Veda wondered.

'All of them were not killed. Only 128 are dead. The rest were cured. I'm sure we will be able to figure out why. But the question remains, who is behind all this? What does he want? Who is the next target? This is getting darker and deeper,' said Vikram still astonished.

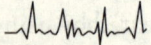

Vikram then got back to his office with all kinds of questions running through his mind. He wanted to break the news to Raghu alone. Just as he reached his office and entered his chamber, Raghu came in running. Before Vikram could even open his mouth, Raghu started: 'Sir, I have some unbelievable findings! Each one of the victims of the mysterious heart disease has a connection with someone who been raided by the IT officials that followed,' Raghu was clearly excited.

'What! Did you check properly?'

'Yes, sir. Please look at this. Pawan Garg, for example, was the auditor of the granite quarry owner; likewise, this office assistant of the textile magnate, who had a heart attack, used to handle accounts for his owner who had been raided later. The same goes with Kiran Kumar, whom you mentioned this morning. He was handling the city group chairman's dirty money. The entire list matches with the other list, sir. This is the most incredible thing I have ever seen in my life,' Raghu exclaimed.

Vikram calmed Raghu down and made him sit down. He was summing up everything that he had found.' You have no idea how deep this is getting! I will explain in a while,' Vikram said as he walked to his seat and sat quietly.

Just then, Ahmed walked in.

'Sir, our informer has some pictures of the chocolate dealer who was handing them out. He has handed over the photos to me,' said Ahmed and gave a sealed envelope to Vikram.

'Put the informer on the line,' Vikram instructed Raghu and started opening the cover. Vikram's hands trembled, as he opened the cover and looked at the pictures. His heart was racing.

'Sir, the informer is on the line,' Raghu handed the phone over to Vikram.

'Sir, his name is Rohan. Rohan Desai. He has been distributing these chocolates under a non-existent brand called Honey Squeeze Chocolates. He has been distributing them at specific places. These photos are from a recent stand-up comedy show, where he had been distributing the chocolates, acting as a sponsor of the event. This event was conducted by the famous stand-up comedian and IAS officer Rakesh.' Vikram's heart was in his mouth.

He looked at the photo in his hand. Rakesh was seen giving a prize to some kid, while Rohan was distributing the chocolates in the background. The photo was taken from the stage.

'How do you know his name is Rohan?' asked Vikram, somehow trying to maintain sanity.

'My wife works there, sir. Rakesh himself had called out his name quite a few times!'

'Oh!' Vikram was shell-shocked.

'One more important thing, sir. Following up on that, I came to know that Rakesh and Rohan have studied in the same school and have been close friends.'

Vikram hung up the phone and took a few deep breaths, absolutely blown away by how things were unfolding in front of him.

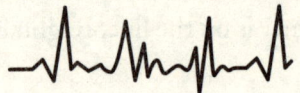

13

Mask. Unmask.

Vikram was dumbfounded by what he had managed to dig up. It was 5 a.m., and he was sitting on his bed motionless, with his hands clasped. He was pondering over the extraordinary circumstances of this case. He took out his phone twice to call Rakesh but somehow managed to curb his instinct.

'It's times like these that one loses faith in the world, in relationships and friendships. A lot of things that I have believed in are falling apart now,' Veda told Vikram, as they jogged together.

'This is mind-boggling,' she kept saying, as Vikram narrated the sequence of events. She felt particularly sorry for Vikram who was feeling dejected on having lost his dear friend.

'You don't lose your good friends, ya. If you lose them then they aren't good enough to be your friends,' she said.

Soon, they were back to their favourite spot at the

municipal corporation park, sipping amla juice.

'I have a few doubts,' started Vikram.

'You can't get this thing off your mind, na?' laughed Veda.

'Not until I get to the very bottom of this. Now, my question is: you said that radio frequency waves break the DNA strands and the toxic drug is released into the body, but how are the radio frequency waves released?' he asked.

'That's simple. Any radio frequency wave-emitting device can be used to activate the drug. For example, something even as simple as a TV remote can activate the drug. There are multiple long-range RF waves emitting devices too,' explained Veda.

'And these waves would not affect the rest of the population, that is, the people who haven't had the chocolates?'

'No, it wouldn't, because these nanoparticles in the chocolates must have been selectively ionized, which, along with iron oxide spheres, selectively attracted the radio frequency waves. Since such selective packaging is done, even if those waves had passed through you or me, nothing would happen to us unless we had the chocolates, selectively packed with the toxic drug or ingredients.'

'Got it. And even if we have had the chocolate, is it harmless unless it has been activated?'

'Yes. This is why only a few people had the heart attacks and related ailments; the whole lot of others, who had eaten the chocolates, did not feel anything and were relatively asymptomatic.'

'So, someone is selectively killing people. It's a brutal medical attack!'

'Yes. A brutal medical attack! Rightly put.'

Vikram went to Veda's hospital for lunch as usual. As he was about to open the door and enter, her assistant came in and said, 'Sir, madam is examining a female patient.'

'Oh, no problem! I'll be in the lobby,' said Vikram and started walking back. Veda's consultation room, where the two met often, was on the first floor. The first floor of the hospital, like every other floor, was in the shape of a cube, with pathways cutting at right angles along its perimeter.

Vikram was about 40 metres away from Veda's room near the stairs. He wanted to use the washroom. He noticed that the public washroom was further away on his right. After taking a couple of right turns, he, finally, found the washroom. As he was about to enter, he saw someone running away frantically in the opposite direction. Vikram immediately ran after him, quickly falling two lefts, and went past the stairs.

It was Rohan. He stood right in front of Veda's room. Rohan was clearly desperate and was trying to figure out his escape. He was a skinny, bony and pale man. He stood at the door in a panic-stricken state, not knowing what to do next.

Veda opened the door that moment and came out with her assistant who had informed her about Vikram's arrival. Vikram immediately pointed at Rohan and shouted, 'Chocolate guy'.

Veda instinctively held him with both her hands. He tried to push her away and hurt her, but by then her assistant came from behind and grappled with Rohan. In a matter of seconds, Vikram was there and struck two blows, one in his face and the other in his stomach. 'This is for hurting Veda now,' he said and hit him the third time, following which Rohan fell down, unconscious.

※

Rohan was taken into police custody. Raghu and Vikram were sitting right opposite Rohan. Vikram gave his usual signal to Raghu. Just when Raghu got up from his seat, the panic-stricken Rohan started giving out information.

His version of the chocolates and the remote-controlled heart attacks almost matched, with what Vikram and Veda had assumed.

'What is Rakesh's role in this?' asked Vikram.

'Just a client,' replied Rohan.

'Client?' both Vikram and Raghu asked in unison.

'Ya, client.'

'Isn't he a good friend of yours? Both of you went

to school and then to college together, didn't you?' asked Vikram.

'Ya, he is a good friend of mine. We both went to school and college together. But can't good friends be clients too?'

'Client for what? Heart attacks? You guys are literally delivering heart attacks to people.' Vikram got up and slapped Rohan hard.

'Sir... Don't beat me... I'm telling you what you want to know!' said Rohan.

Vikram got up and slapped him again. 'Now tell me properly. What business is this? You create heart attacks in people. Your clients direct you to the next victim, is it?'

'Yes, except the fact that heart attacks are only one part of it!'

'One part? What the f@#* is the other part?'

'Information! We deal with information extraction using bio nano chips!'

'Oh my god! What the hell!'

'Is this biochip a part of the drug too?' asked Vikram.

'Yes,' replied Rohan.

'Then tell me the complete configuration.'

'It's a part of the complex—drug-DNA-iron spheres. On one side of the DNA, the iron spheres are connected to the drug, and on its other side, the iron spheres are connected to the biochip. The DNA acts as a binding agent for both sides. The DNA is tightly packed with the drug, and on the biochip side, the DNA and the iron spheres are loosely packed,' replied Rohan.

'This means...?' Raghu was unable to understand.

'This means we can apply RF waves at two frequencies, which will heat up the complex variably,' said Rohan.

'What happens then?' asked Vikram.

'The looser DNA strands break first and the biochip is activated. This is stage one. Once the biochip is activated, it just acts as a transmitter, which sends sound waves through the same RF waves. Then, we receive the feed through our speakers,' he said.

'Basically, you are implanting a recording device inside a person, which gets activated with heat and transmits sounds through RF waves. You listen to the conversations through a speaker with the help of these waves,' confirmed Vikram.

'Ya,' Rohan seemed disappointed now that the secret was out.

He seemed timid. Clearly, he didn't want to fight Raghu and Vikram. It seemed like he just wanted to tell everything and get done with it. He would be sentenced to a few years in jail as punishment. He still had a lot of money to lead a happy and luxurious life abroad after serving his sentence.

'Even if I resist, these guys are gonna beat the sh*# out of me,' he thought.

'Now what is the second stage?' asked Vikram.

'You already know that. The heart attack!' replied Rohan.

'So stage one is the extraction of information and stage two is the heart attack,' Raghu confirmed.

'Yes, but technically, prolonged information extraction breaks the other DNA chain too and leads to heart attacks or heart-related issues,' said Rohan.

'How do you send the targeted RF waves?' asked Vikram.

'We place our van at close proximity to the subject and then start the process. The blue button is for stage one and the red one is for stage two.'

'How simple! And what about your chocolate van? Is that your crime factory?' Vikram was still surprised. 'Can other RF waves interfere and activate the complex, after the people have eaten the chocolates?'

'No. Highly unlikely. Iron spheres are set in such a way that only concentrated high-intensity RF waves heat them up. So, other RF waves from appliances or accidental exposure to these waves do not activate the complex,' said Rohan.

'You think you are an expert on this, no?' Vikram slapped him again. He couldn't contain his anger.

'Hydra! He is the professor...principal...everything!' exclaimed a frenzied Rohan.

'They have made a business out of it,' said Vikram.

He had just finished telling the entire story to Veda.

'Hydra is the kingpin of this game. He seems to be an information agent and a modern-day assassin,' said Vikram.

'Modern-day assassin, plus an information agent, plus an entrepreneur,' said Veda.

'Yes, actually! This is their first venture in India. They have tried a few similar ventures in Bangkok and Phnom Penh,' admitted Vikram.

'And what is with this name—Hydra! It sounds like an organism or a technology!' Veda remarked.

'And these 200-odd people, who were affected, were mostly, as we guessed, money handlers of the rich, managing their dirty money. They were "bio-tapped", and "IT raided" later! In certain cases, the bigger fishes were directly tapped and raided!' said Vikram.

'That is actually a spine-chilling act of a genius! But who is behind the whole thing?' asked Veda.

'Rakesh! He was their client for all the events in Laxmipur. There is an official admission by Rohan!'

'What does Rakesh gain out of this? You think he spied on these people and sent info to the IT department? Why is he so hell-bent on cleaning up black money?'

'Whatever the reason may be, he has committed serious crimes, and there is enough evidence to substantiate them—playbacks from their biochips, samples of the chocolates that they distributed, their contents, numerous witnesses who received the chocolates, CCTV footages confirming the same, a phone call between Rakesh and Rohan, and lastly, Rohan's admission. I have everything ready to get a sanction for prosecution against Rakesh!'

'Oh my god! He is an IAS officer. Are IAS officers arrested? I mean…they are so powerful!' replied Veda.

'These days, IAS officers are arrested even for things they haven't done. Their crime is that they are IAS officers. Others in power, craving for power, thrown out of power, those who never had power but want to become powerful the wrong way, assume that IAS officers are powerful and target them just to bring them down. I know quite a few sincere IAS officers, falling prey to anything from political vendetta to publicity politics! When such sincere officers are treated with disdain for something that they have never done, there is nothing wrong in getting scoundrels like Rakesh thrashed,' said Vikram.

Just then, his phone rang.

'VK! How are you?' the voice from the other end sounded familiar.

'I'm good, Rakesh. What is up with you?' he said.

'I'm leaving for London tonight for a stand-up show. This will be my first show abroad. It's gonna be awesome. I'm so excited. I wanted to tell you, bro,' said Rakesh.

'Oh great! All the best, Rakesh! When is the show?' asked Vikram.

'Tomorrow evening. I'm starting from Delhi tonight and reaching London tomorrow morning,' he said.

'Great! Happy journey! I will watch the show online,' said Vikram and hung up.

'Rakesh doesn't know yet! It's been four hours since we

caught Rohan and nobody knows a thing except you, me and Raghu. The local police think it's a molestation case!'

'Whom did he molest?'

'You.'

'Heyyyyyyyyyy! What have you done? You should have told me before filing the charges against him!'

'You signed a paper, baby! That was basically your complaint! Anyway, leave all that to me. That is just a complaint, and everyone is under the impression that I'm personally looking into the matter, since he had tried to molest my girlfriend. That's why the media has been keeping quiet. I don't know how long it will be before the news gets out. We need to stop Rakesh from going out of India, and punish him. I need to do three things immediately. One, obtain a prosecution sanction against Rakesh; two, rush to Delhi on the next flight, and three...' Vikram stopped as he got a bit tense.

'What's the third? Come on...tell me!'

'I need to eat a a honey squeeze chocolate.'

'WHAT!'

14

Unplotted

Vikram breathed heavily, as he held the chocolate in his hand, mustering courage to have it.

'Raghu has taken possession of the van. We have taken out the long-range RF-emitting system from it. Raghu is travelling with me to Delhi. He will be in the van, with the equipment, outside the airport and push the blue button once I enter the airport to meet Rakesh. The biochip will get activated and emit sounds back to Raghu's device, which will be recorded. Despite all the evidences we have, there is nothing more concrete than Rakesh's admission to his crimes,' said Vikram.

'There are easier ways of doing it. A simple spycam would do. Do you want to risk your life for this?' Veda was truly scared.

'See, we are going to document how the whole thing plays out. That is the strongest evidence we can create, which will rattle even the most powerful people. This is going to be the biggest sting operation ever!' said Vikram.

'And Raghu will only press the blue button. Going by their algorithm that will activate only the biochip,' he continued.

'Do you really trust their algorithm? Many have suffered from the adverse effects of their manoeuvres. Why should you risk your life, ya? Please don't!'

'No, Veda. It's very important to trap them in their own game! Apart from the chocolate, a spy cam in my pen will send the live feed to Raghu. Another cam will capture the live feed from Raghu and the device. Both the feeds will be integrated into one footage, explaining how the whole thing is supposed to work. That evidence will speak for itself—from the government to the court.'

Vikram briefly paused and then said, 'I love you, Veda,' and swallowed the chocolate. 'It tastes awful!'

He tried to crack a joke as tears rolled down Veda's eyes. She tried to smile but couldn't. She hugged Vikram tightly. Her tears seeped through Vikram's shirt onto his chest.

The IGIA departure terminal was buzzing with activity. Cars jammed the path so closely that there was no space for pedestrians to move. Rakesh struggled to reach the entrance of the departure terminal. He flashed his ID card at the security guard, along with his ticket, and walked in.

Vikram and Raghu, meanwhile, had just landed in Delhi at the other terminal.

Rakesh tried printing his boarding pass at the automatic kiosk. There was a continuous noise in the machine, and the boarding pass would just not pop out. Rakesh queued up at a check-in counter.

Vikram and Raghu were rushing towards Rakesh's departure terminal.

'Why don't we call him once, sir? We might lose him,' said Raghu.

'Rakesh is shrewd. He will deduce immediately. That's a huge risk,' replied Vikram.

'We will lose him in 10 minutes, sir. We must do something,' urged Raghu.

Meanwhile, Rakesh got his boarding pass and proceeded towards security check.

Vikram navigated through the parked vehicles, jumped over luggage, and somehow reached the entrance. He flashed his ID card.

'Sorry, sir, we cannot let you in without a ticket,' said the guard firmly.

'So much for all the hue and cry over IAS *babu*-dom,' he said to himself and pulled out his phone.

'Hello! Oh! But you never said that...' Rakesh started panicking after the call. He tried to rush through the line and get his security check done as quickly as possible.

Vikram, meanwhile, was getting anxious and dialling numbers frantically. His heart was palpitating. It had been about 15 minutes since the drug in him had been activated, and Vikram was feeling the effects. He was still at the gate waiting to be let in.

Rakesh breathed a sigh of relief as he reached the frisking zone. The guard started frisking him and was about to put the seal on his boarding pass when their commandant walked in.

'Stop,' he called out sharply to the guard who restrained himself from stamping the seal.

'Sir! You cannot pass through! You have been summoned to the departure waiting lounge,' said the commandant.

'What? I am an IAS officer! How dare you!' started Rakesh, trying to sound furious, but he was actually scared. 'I'm royally screwed,' he thought.

'There has been a prosecution sanction against you, and I have been instructed to bring you to the departure lounge. Here is the copy of it. I received the fax moments ago,' said the commandant.

Vikram got his clearance to enter. He got a call from Raghu.

'Sir, I have mailed the prosecution sanction order to the commandant and have asked him to bring Rakesh to the lounge. Just got a confirmation that he has been stopped from completing the security check. A couple of our people are already waiting for him. They will take over as soon as you have completed your interrogation,' said Raghu.

'Wow! That is really smart, Raghu. But how did you know that I hadn't got in yet?'

'Ha Ha! You are being tracked now. I heard your conversations at the gate clearly, including all the cuss words for Rakesh!' said Raghu. 'I hope the side effects aren't too evident yet?'

'I do have an unusual feeling in my chest. Will try to wrap up the interrogation asap,' said Vikram as he walked into the departure lounge.

'Oh okay, take care, sir. Do call out if the situation gets out of hand. I will stop the transmission. We can't risk anything happening to you,' said Raghu.

The commandant and Rakesh were already in the lounge, as the Laxmipur police officially took over Rakesh.

On Vikram's orders, the police officers went out, along with the commandant, leaving Rakesh and Vikram in the lounge.

'So! Rakesh! I stop you yet again from running away!' said Vikram. 'But this time, I am not going to advise you or convince you. You have dug your own grave,' Vikram continued.

'What do you mean...' started Rakesh.

'Oh! Please! Can you come to the point? Do you think we will get a warrant against you just like that? Rohan has told us everything,' said Vikram.

'Rohan?' the very mention of the name sent shivers down his spine.

'So arrest me! Go on!' said Rakesh in a fevered tone.

'Why Rakesh? God gave you an awesome job. He gave you a special talent too. You have squandered away a wonderful life,' said Vikram.

'Please stop this. You know what? You remember what you told me the other night when I had tried to run away from LBSNAA? It would be easier to promote myself as a stand-up artist after I had become an IAS officer?' reminded Rakesh. He sounded extremely bull-headed, although he felt broken within.

'Yeah. I said that to convince you to stay back,' replied Vikram.

'What you said was actually correct and practical. Someone just told me to add money to that equation. I saw a new future for myself, where I could even produce my shows and go global in a short time!' said Rakesh

'And that someone was RPR, right?' Vikram asked. Vikram had guessed RPR's involvement; he knew RPR was the one to benefit the most out of the entire situation. Vikram was feeling numb and anosmic. He felt his nose and found that he was bleeding.

'I'm stopping the transmission in exactly three minutes,' said Raghu.

Rakesh kept quiet.

'See, I know it, and you know it too. Just tell me the name of the person behind all this. I have enough evidence to lock him up,' said Vikram in the nastiest possible way, intimidating Rakesh.

'Do you remember that day outside the director's office in LBSNAA when you were threatened and were crying? That broke me completely. You were my hero until then, and to see "my hero" being destroyed made me lose even the slightest hope in this service. I found my new hero in RPR, who effortlessly broke you down. I didn't want what happened to your family to happen to mine. I fell at his feet, and he accepted me with open arms,' said Rakesh.

It had always been easy for him to confide into Vikram, which made it impossible for Rakesh to hold back anything from Vikram.

'RPR has been treating me like his brother since then. Over the past one year, you must have noticed how much I have grown as a stand-up artist. I'm one of the biggest entertainment superstars in the country living my dream now. It's all because of him,' said Rakesh.

'And you, in turn, helped him with his dirty work—giving him the list of people handling black money and helping him take down his enemies.'

'I was only acting as his interface for Hydra's team and RPR. They extracted information about black money holders in Laxmipur, which I gave to RPR. He used his influence in Delhi and made those raids happen. Everyone, who was likely to use their money to fund other parties or play a role against him in the elections, was raided. He then ensured that Hydra killed Rakhi and Nandan, who had been threatening to withdraw their support from RPR. He offered them money too, but they refused to budge as they had their own political plans in mind. So, he doctored the riot!' laughed Rakesh.

'What about Pandey?'

'Pandey was actually the CM's candidate to contest against RPR in Laxmipur, again. It was the CM's masterplan to bring back Pandey, whom everyone respected, to phase out RPR. With the help of raids, orchestrating the riots and taking out Pandey, RPR ensured that he retained his supremacy and that his enemies were financially weak before the elections. He is now all set for an emphatic victory and is making his move to become the deputy chief minister once he wins the elections.'

'What about the Everest Factory?' asked Vikram, enduring the pain.

'That was his ploy to divert the public's attention from the heart attacks and the medicine board to close the case. He was extremely pissed that you weren't doing as he asked of you. He had been planning something really nasty against you before the orders were passed.'

Vikram was losing consciousness now. His heart was pounding. He had started bleeding profusely from the nose and ears. Rakesh saw Vikram bleeding and realized that he had been trapped in his own game! He started panicking, not knowing what to do.

Raghu had just stopped the transmission. But Vikram

continued to bleed profusely and was in severe pain. He could hardly talk. Hearing the noise, the police officials rushed in.

'You recorded and transmitted everything I said!' Rakesh realized what had just happened.

'Of course!' Vikram gathered all his strength to deliver his final punch. 'This transmission will reach everyone, including RPR. He will destroy you completely now. He will destroy your family too,' Vikram fell down.

Raghu ran into the lounge with the airport emergency medical team. They picked up Vikram and moved him to the emergency room.

Rakesh was hysterical and didn't know what to do. He shouted at the top of his voice, snatched a revolver from one of the police officers standing nearby, and aimed it at them. Suddenly, he got scared, pointed the gun at himself and pulled the trigger.

'Bang!'

The bullet went straight into his skull and he fell down motionless. His eyes were wide open, aghast and shell-shocked. They gave away an unmissable story of greed that was born out of wrongdoings and desperation to realize a dream.

Rakesh had just run away from the toughest situation of his life. This time there wasn't a Vikram to bring him back.

Vikram opened his eyes after an hour. Raghu was by his side.

'Thankfully, you stopped the transmission at the right time,' said Vikram with a smile.

'Rakesh is dead. Shot himself. The entire country is talking about this now,' said Raghu.

'Oh! It is a pity I wasn't there to stop him this time. His dream and passion were true, but the means he chose to achieve them weren't. Wherever there is greed, there is always trouble!' said Vikram calmly.

'Can we leave now?' he asked Raghu.

'As soon as the chief doctor discharges me,' said Raghu.

'Have you ever seen RPR scared and jittery?'

'No.'

'You will see that soon. Our time is now! Call the Election Commisson,' said Vikram with a smile as he got up from the bed.

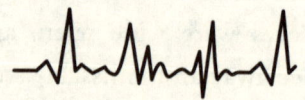

15

Face Off—The Final

This was the day Vikram had been impatiently waiting for. He had been humiliated, had endured unbearable stress, and he had been dreaming about this day every single day. He wanted to pin RPR down and have the last laugh, and that opportunity was right in front of him.

Vikram and Raghu were on their flight back to Laxmipur. They were seated, and the in-flight safety instructions were being given.

'Have you spoken to the Election Commission, sir?'

'Yes! I have spoken to them and have sent across all the evidence available us, including the audio feed from my conversation with Rakesh today. They will surely take strong action.'

'Okay, sir.'

'Also, I spoke to the chief secretary and the DGP, and sent them all the evidence and reports too. We can expect massive news soon!'

'Awesome, sir!'

'But I don't want to stop here! This is the biggest opportunity to break him completely, and I don't want to take any chances.'

'So, what now, sir?'

'Ha ha! The world is a click away, Raghu!' said Vikram. He was extremely tired, worn-out and weak. Yet, he seemed his strongest and was pumped-up for what was to be the final face off with RPR.

He collected all the evidence, starting with the report on the chocolates, post-mortems, voice extract files, which had his conversations with Rakesh, and put them into a single folder in his phone. Vikram then attached the folder to his mail and hit the 'Send to all' button from an anonymous mail ID.

'Whooooosh!' RPR is going to become famous across the world! I have just mailed everything to all the media houses,' said Vikram, as their flight took off.

A couple of hours later, they landed at the Laxmipur airport. As they were waiting for their luggage, they saw RPR's face on every television set, with the breaking-news banner flashing from corner to corner.

'The party high command has removed Rudra Pratap Rana from his candidature in Laxmipur West MLA constituency. The party has issued a press release, stating that the new candidate from Laxmipur West will be announced in a couple of days,' was the hottest news on one half of the screen. The other half of the screen was, as expected, occupied by the audio tapes and transcripts that Vikram had sent.

By the time Vikram and Raghu picked up their luggage and were walking out, news broke that RPR had been sacked from all party posts, including primary membership of the party.

There were also scrolls going around stating that the Election Commission and the police department had taken cognizance of the matter and would initiate their proceedings soon.

Vikram carried his luggage and walked out of the airport with a smile. Veda was waiting for him. He walked up to her, hugged and kissed her.

'You see that place? He pointed at the carousel and said, 'It was there that VK had been waiting for his bags, and RPR lost his candidature.'

'Ha ha,' Veda laughed.

Vikram continued, 'It was there that VK picked up his bags and was leaving, when RPR lost his place in the party.'

Vikram was reminiscing with Veda about one of their first-ever conversations trolling RPR.

Raghu, who had been on the phone all the while, walked up to them and said, 'A warrant has been issued against RPR. He will be taken into custody soon. SP and DM Mahadev are at his residence now. RPR is making them wait by telling them that he is on the phone with somebody important, sorting things out,' said Raghu.

'Let's go there straight,' said Vikram, waving at Veda.

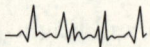

RPR was fuming, with the phone in his hand.

'Will you get me out of this or not?' he was yelling at the CM at the top of his voice.

'See, things have gone beyond our reach. Did you ask me before doing these things? Now the Election Commission has initiated action. The media is tearing the party apart. The public is watching and we are going to the polls next month! What do you want me to do now—refute the allegations as usual and say that the tapes are doctored? Then that SDM Vikram will do another live demo with me next! There is very little we can do now,' said the voice on the other end.

'So are you going to throw me out of the party? All of my followers will walk out. You will not get a single seat in this region.'

'Having you in the party will not get us a single seat in the entire state. Now, I can claim that the party has dealt with such corrupt people in a strong way and end this issue. I have asked one of the new actors to release a scandalous recording of a director to divert the media's attention. Once that comes out and you are in custody, this will slowly die out. Next week onwards, I will start announcing election sops and freebies. I'm still confident of winning this time. Once we win, I'll dilute the investigation and set you free,' said the CM, who, in his mind, was chuffed to get rid of the dangerous RPR.

'I should have sent you the chocolates first,' RPR erupted again, hung up, threw the phone and walked out of his room.

Vikram was standing outside his room, like a fearsome tiger, right in front of RPR, and looked deep into his eyes. He had got out of the hospital a few hours ago, standing tall and full of vengeance. On one side of Vikram was Raghu and on the other side was the SP. Mahadev was still scared and confused. He was hiding somewhere behind them.

'What if Mantriji comes back after this ends?' he kept asking himself.

SP started the arrest procedure and got ready to take RPR into his custody. RPR gave out one final loud roar and started walking with the SP.

'All of you! Just see what I do to all of you. I will finish every last one of you!' he grunted.

His sidekick went running to him and whispered that Vikram was recording everything.

RPR glared at Vikram and kept walking. Vikram kept quiet. He walked behind the police officers and RPR.

Mahadev didn't really know how to react as they walked past him. 'Good morning, sir,' he blurted, as he habitually did.

RPR was taken into the jeep and through the streets of Laxmipur. The very streets of the city that he considered his own. It was still early morning, yet people were gathered in large numbers to catch a glimpse of RPR being taken away by the police.

'Serves him right! I knew this day would come,' said a few, while some said, 'Who will give us money and freebies now?'

The men from his party didn't know how to respond. They were too shocked to respond, although quite a few of them tried to block the vehicle, pelted stones, etc., at the police and were arrested by the armed reserve forces who had been trailing behind RPR's jeep.

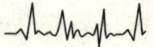

RPR was made to sit on a bench placed right in the middle of an otherwise empty room. There were no windows in it. A couple of dimly lit bulbs lighted the room, and it seemed like it was night. Vikram, Raghu, SP and Mahadev were the other people in the room.

'Before the police department begins its official proceedings. I wish to say a few things,' said Vikram, clearing his throat.

'Sure Vikram, go ahead,' said the SP.

'Do you know the greatest form of humiliation? It's seeing how powerful your enemy is day in and day out and realizing your impotence to go against him! That feeling is the greatest humiliation! That is worse than death! You will now feel it every single day!' said Vikram. Those had been RPR's exact words to Vikram. 'You hear that?' Vikram growled at the top of his voice.

RPR didn't say anything. By then, his body language had completely changed. He was sitting submissively, without uttering a word.

'The respect we give to people like you and the allegiance we pledge towards you is NOT suitable for you! It is for the people—every single one of them who have waited in queues and elected you. It is not right for you to disrespect us our subordination!' said Vikram rather emotionally. 'When you abuse us, when you try to crush us, there may be a few people like Rakesh whom you are able to corrupt and have them side with you, and a few like Jaidev, who run away from the system or lose hope in it. But there are thousands of Vikrams out there—fighting within the system—to protect and save it from people like you. In this fight, we may lose our families, we may lose our friends, we may even lose our reputation, but the only thing that we don't lose is hope! Every time you abuse us, we stand up and fight. That is the pride and the magic of those letters behind our names. Nothing f#*@ing else!' Vikram let his heart out. Raghu, SP and even Mahadev were overwhelmed and had goosebumps on their arms. 'My family was humiliated, and my sister's nine-month-old baby killed in her womb. Did I run away? Did I side with you? Did I sit and cry helplessly? I stood up and fought! And fought by being in this system because I trust it. I love this country and its system. At least learn now!

Stop manipulating the system! Try to become the leader people really want you to be!' Vikram's eyes were brimming with tears as he finished speaking.

RPR sat silently with his head hanging.

Suddenly, in a tremendous fit of rage, Vikram stepped forward, moved the table separating them and kicked RPR his chest. RPR lost his balance and flew into the wall. He fell with a loud thud.

'That was for the baby,' said Vikram, as he walked out of the room and slammed the door.

It had been a few days since RPR had been arrested. A special court had accepted all the evidence given by the Laxmipur police and had ordered for a special investigation team to probe the matter from beginning to end. RPR had kept in police custody till then. He had been also barred from contesting the elections. A special police team had been formed to seize Hydra, the supposed leader of Rohan's gang. Despite engaging a lot of men and machinery, they had been unable to find anything about Hydra.

Vikram and Raghu were now standing in front of Rohan in his cell. He had just finished eating his meal.

'Rohan, you know what? You are very clever!' started Vikram.

Rohan started at him blankly.

'After RPR's arrest, I heard the tape between me and Rakesh. Not once has he mentioned your name, despite you handling everything and being his friend through school and college. All he mentioned was Hydra who is nowhere to be found. Then I checked your records from school and college. Traced the address and secretly enquired in your family to find that you, i.e. Rohan, died four years ago in a road accident. I also have the FIR copies and relevant documents to support it,' declared Vikram.

'This...' Vikram pulled out a picture from his pocket, 'is the original picture of Rohan,' he declared.

'Then who the hell is this guy in front of us, sir?' asked Raghu in shock.

'Tell him... Tell him, man... That you are Hyder, a.k.a. Hydra! And how you, Rakesh and Rohan, went to the same college, and how you conveniently assumed Rohan's identity after his death.'

'Holy s#*t! This is unbelievable!' cried Raghu.

'Yes, I'm Hyder, a.k.a. Hydra. Rakesh, Rohan and I went to the same medical college. I had become a drug addict, and midway through college, I was thrown out for smuggling drugs through chocolates and selling them. I also got arrested.'

'Yes, I have the copy of the FIR with me,' said Vikram.

'I was deeply angry with the system as my career were completely ruined and my dreams of becoming the greatest ever doctor were crushed. I then started studying on my own, without even going to college. My thirst to study knew no limits when I battled my urges and frustrations. I studied everything—medicine, computers, electronics… literally everything that came my way. My frustration and fetish for studies turned me into a knowledge maniac! I wanted to create something super powerful and satiate my frustration. Hence, I created the instrument for the ultimate information extraction and, a killing machine. After Rohan died, I assumed his identity for paperwork.'

'You knew well that you were caught on camera, didn't you? That's when you came to Blue Line Hospital'.

'Yes. The boss of City Group of Hospitals sided with RPR after the raids. I was then referred to him for my hideout, as you were creating trouble and things were getting out of hand. I then decided to undergo plastic surgery and change my face to assume a new Identity. My bad luck that you saw me that very day!'

'And after you were caught, you posed as Rohan, thought you would keep up with the lies, become a witness for prosecution, somehow get out of trial and anyway go ahead with the surgery and start a new life! Isn't it?'

'Yes, and I dare you to stop me! Eventually, that is what I'm going to do! What will you do? I have even told my entire story now. You can hold me now, but no man can stop me forever! I have beat the system, and I will keep beating the system again and again and again!' said Hydra in a challenging tone. 'I'm a monster of knowledge! I can create a hundred RPRs, destroy a hundred Vikrams! Do what you can, conduct your enquiries; I know how to escape. I have influence around the globe.'

'Exactly! That's the problem, Mr Hyder, a.k.a. Hydra! You know how to escape, and it's not going to happen.'

'Meaning?' asked Hydra.

Vikram started smiling as Hydra started bleeding from his eyes and nose.

'I'm not a knowledge monster or a maniac, but an average government servant who can skillfully replicate things! What did you have before I came in? Aloo parathas? If you can play with chocolates, I can play with aloo parathas. The transmission is on! Rest in peace!'

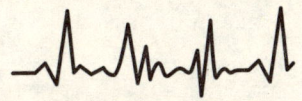

Epilogue

A few months later...

The ruling party had lost the assembly elections that followed. RPR's trial was still on. Nobody was able to make out what was on RPR's mind, as he refused to meet anybody, and led a reclusive life in jail. The entire heart attack and RPR episode had shook the nation over these few months. There were so many theories and counter-theories coming up, especially over Rakesh and Hyder's deaths. Vikram was acclaimed for all his work. Bollywood had even started making a biopic on him!

Mahadev, finally, ceased to be a DM and was transferred to the state secretariat. He tried his best to avoid his transfer and spend the rest of his career as DM, but all his efforts were in vain.

The dean published a paper on the clinical data and the disease based on the incidents of Laxmipur, and won international recognition even with his mediocre work.

Jaidev was becoming more anti-establishment or

anti-government, and a bigger rebel by the day. He had a national presence now.

'Karan…let's name him Karan,' said Vikram, as he lifted the baby and kissed him.

'Don't kiss him! You may pass on germs to him! Doctor has told us to be careful,' Vikram's mother gave him a friendly warning.

Vikram kept kissing the baby, paying no heed to what his mother said.

'When has he ever listened to you, Padma?' laughed Vikram's father.

'I know you have always wanted to name your son Karan, and I also know that's the name of your high school crush and tuition mate,' Vikram laughed loudly.

His sister Swetha was just recovering from the anesthetic effects of a caesarian section and still managed a scowl on her face and told Vikram to shut up.

'Who is your crush and sweetheart, bro?' Swetha's husband, Sidharth, joined in the banter.

'Where there is a Vikram, there is always be a Veda and their amla tree!' Swetha didn't shy away from teasing Vikram, despite her surgical pain.

'So, when are you two getting married?' asked Gaurav, Vikram's father.

'Well, you have got to tell us that, pa,' Vikram was beating about the bush.

'He is lying! As if he is waiting for your permission! He is a liar, pa. Veda is in the UK now,' said Swetha.

'Okay, let me find out myself,' Vikram's dad took out the phone.

Swetha gave him Veda's number and Gaurav made a FaceTime call.

'Oh my god! You people!' Vikram felt shy and nervous.

Veda appeared on the other end. She was sitting on a desk with some book in her hand. They could hear her Timmy in the background.

Gaurav looked at the screen. On her wall was a photo collage—a collage of numerous pictures of Vikram. Gaurav gave a hearty and contented smile and straightaway asked her, 'When are you marrying my son?'

Veda could not stop blushing. She went off camera for a while and then returned.

'As soon as I'm done with this course, uncle! And as soon as Vikram completes his tenure in his current assignment. Both are likely to happen in a month and a half!' Veda sounded excited as she spoke those words.

'Okay, okay! Come back soon! We can't wait any longer!'

'Yes, uncle! My love to the entire family.'

Gaurav was about to hang up after waving at her.

'Uncle! Uncle!' she called out.

'What is it, Veda?'

'Just tell Vikram to stop flirting with that nurse at the hospital, and please remind him that I hold the patents for RF-based remote-controlled cardiovascular treatments,' she joked.

It was another cold, dark, October night in Mussoorie. Vikram was attending his batch's reunion at LBSNAA. It was only a few days until Veda arrived and their wedding was only a few weeks away.

'These reunions are exciting, ma'am,' said Shamitha to the course coordinator as she took her place at the outdoor amphitheater. It was only five minutes ago that she had cribbed to her friends about how boring these events were and how they only helped people boast about themselves.

'Welcome back to the academy,' said the course coordinator amidst roars from the audience, which comprised Vikram's batchmates.

'Let's get started with tonight's event. One by one, walk up to the stage and tell one great thing that you have achieved from the time you left the academy and started on your independent paths. The stage is all yours,' said the course coordinator.

This was the day Shankar had been waiting for! In fact, he had written a speech about his achievements on his flight to Dehradun. There were cries and catcalls as he went on bragging about himself for over ten minutes.

'I said "one big achievement"!' said the coordinator and asked him to come down the stage.

There were truly inspiring stories from a lot of the officers—from fighting the sand mafia to releasing children from bonded labour. These were truly uplifting and soul satisfying stories.

There were laugh riots.

Then Shamitha took to the stage and started being too humble and spoke about everything. There were murmurs and chuckles in the audience.

The entire crowd was in splits when Kamya walked up audaciously and told that her biggest achievement in her career so far was an awareness video, where she had spoken pre-written lines about how movies were spoiling Indian values and culture, and how there was a huge response from Bollywood to her video, stating that they would make socially responsible movies henceforth.

Soon it was Vikram's turn to walk onto the stage. He walked in as casual as always. He stood there, took a deep breath and smiled. The silent crowd started clapping, which rose to a crescendo of cheers and a long heart-warming standing ovation!

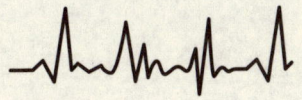